DOG ON THE CROSS

DOG ON THE CROSS

stories by **AARON GWYN**

ALGONQUIN BOOKS OF

CHAPEL HILL

2004

Published by
ALGONQUIN BOOKS OF CHAPEL HILL
Post Office Box 2225
Chapel Hill, North Carolina 27515-2225

a division of
Workman Publishing
708 Broadway
New York, New York 10003

Portions of this book have appeared in slightly different
versions in the following publications: "Of Falling" and
"Dog on the Cross," *Louisiana Literature;* "Truck," *Black
Warrior Review;* "In Tongues," *American Literary Review;*
"The Backsliders" and "Offering," *Glimmer Train;* and
"Courtship," *Texas Review.* "Of Falling" was reprinted
in *New Stories from the South: The Year's Best, 2002.*

Library of Congress Cataloging-in-Publication Data
Gwyn, Aaron.
Dog on the cross : stories / by Aaron Gwyn.—1st ed.
p. cm.
Contents: Of falling — Courtship — The offering —
Against the pricks — Truck — In tongues — The
backsliders — Dog on the cross.
ISBN 1-56512-412-X
1. Oklahoma—Social life and customs—Fiction.
2. Pentecostal churches—Fiction.   3. Pentecostals—
Fiction.   4. Healers—Fiction.   I. Title.
PS3607.W96D64 2004
813'.54—dc22   2003066445

10   9   8   7   6   5   4   3   2   1
First Edition

FOR MARK,

nos haec novimus esse nihil

"If you would pray," the old lady said,
"Jesus would help you."
"That's right," The Misfit said.

—FLANNERY O'CONNOR,
"A Good Man Is Hard to Find"

CONTENTS

DOG ON THE CROSS

OF FALLING

GEORGE CRIDER WAS seven when Freddy was born, fifteen before his brother grew old enough to sit a horse. In the autumn, after their chores were done, the boys would ride bareback across the pasture to a persimmon grove, spend their afternoons climbing the thin trees for fruit.

One day the animal they were riding stepped in a sinkhole and bucked. George caught hold of its mane, but his brother was behind him and fell to the ground. The boy's arm broke the skin, and the bone jutted into dirt. He developed tetanus and in two weeks was dead. George blamed himself for this, as did his parents, and at the funeral, when he climbed into the grave and sought to open the casket, his father lost two teeth trying to retrieve him.

Three years later, grown to well over six feet, he slid a razor in his hip pocket, a change of clothes in his knapsack, and without saying good-bye, walked forty miles through the Quashita forest until he came to Highway 3, hitching across Oklahoma in the back of a cattle truck. He went to work in the oil field and bought a new car, kept a shotgun underneath his seat, sawed at the stock and barrel. One night he left for Louisiana and returned a week later with a Cajun woman, named Sadie, whom he had taken to wife.

Everyone thought George unflappable. He was tall and lean, with a hard, lean face and expressionless eyes. He did not talk about himself or his brother or his parents back in Shinewell, pastors of a Pentecostal church. He was quiet and felt no need to speak. The men he worked with respected him, for they knew he was strong and stubborn, and they would not have wanted to face him in a fight, fair or otherwise.

Then, in 1933, working the eighth floor of an oil derrick in Pontotoc County, scaffolding gave way and George fell 116 feet onto the bank of a saltwater pit.

He did not remember this. Not the fabric blowing against his limbs or the girders moving past or the platform where he'd stood traveling into sky. It took him nearly four seconds to reach the ground, but he could not recall them. For him there was only the eighth floor and the earth.

Through the years to follow, he would recount

the incident for his wife: the stares of the men who found him, the ambulance and hospital, the doctor who examined him from top to toe as if he were a puzzle. He would tell her about watching the clouds change to ceiling tile, the sun to bright lamps and mirrors. He would tell about sandstone pressing into his back like shards of bone and then the cool of the sheets, the anesthetic.

Yet, stretched beneath the shadow of the derrick, George's first thoughts were not of family or friends, the condition of his soul, or whether he would be able to one day move his legs. His thoughts were not of the porch standing unfinished, the clothesline needing repair, the foundation wall that had shown signs of flaking just the day before. His thoughts were not of what he would lose in this world, gain or lose in the world hereafter.

Lying there with the sky weighing down and the wind moving over and across him, George had considered only the boards that had snapped beneath his feet. With his lower lip clenched between his teeth, he watched himself walk to where they lay at the side of the derrick and kick them to splinters.

THE FALL HAD broken both his arms, his legs, six of his ribs at their connecting points. His skull was fractured, and his sternum snapped in half. The doctor who admitted him said he would not live through the night.

He lived regardless. Through that night and the night after and the night after that.

The surgeons said it was a wonder; they said it was a phenomenon. One stood in the middle of his hospital room and pronounced it a miracle. And though he said George would never walk, he thought he might, one day, have a life of some kind.

In two years George was walking. In two more he had returned to work. By the time he reached his midthirties, George was spry as any roughneck in the state. He was promoted to foreman, and through the depression years, when many left to seek work elsewhere, George and his wife began to build a collection of antique glassware. If he chose, he could retire young, live comfortably off his pension and what he had invested in glass rarities.

George seemed much the same as before the fall. To see him pull to the curb in his burgundy Pontiac, step out and approach an antique shop—a tall, slender man, graceful as a dancer, with jet-black hair and eyes like drops of oil—you would not have thought he had fallen in his life. Not even from the height of a chair.

IT WAS ALONG this time, along the time George stacked his crutches in the rear of the closet and poured his vial of laudanum down the sink, that the dreams came.

They were not, as one would think, dreams of

falling, the body released from its federation with the earth and betrayed to gravity. Neither were they dreams of impact. The dreams that visited George after his fall were of stillness.

In them, he would be lying in a field, feeling drops of sweat run into his eyes and pool around the sockets. When he attempted to raise his hand and wipe them, he could not. His ears itched, his face and neck. His body burned. He lay among the blades of grass, blinking into sky.

Soon there was a cloud. It was small at first. If he had been able, George could have retrieved a quarter from his pocket, held it at arm's length, and eclipsed the cloud entirely. But as it grew, he would have needed a fifty-cent piece, a silver dollar, and then, even with both hands outspread and extended in front of his face, wisps of gray would have bled the edges of his fingers.

There was nothing about the cloud to warrant fear. It was not boiling and black, or streaked with light. There was no rumbling and it gave no sound. This was not the type of cloud from which angels or prophets descend.

Only, lying there beneath it, George came to know death in the stillness of wide and all but empty sky.

He awoke screaming. He awoke on the floor. The doctors said such dreams were common among those who had fallen. They gave him pills of all sizes, but the dreams did not stop.

Then one night he awoke running through the house, glassware rattling the mahogany furniture. Sadie watched him from their doorway.

"Crider," she called, "you'll break everything we own."

She was right; several vases lay broken already.

When he wakened and was asked what he'd been dreaming, George went to his car and fell asleep across the seats. The next morning, he was sitting on the front stoop of Woolworth when the owner unlocked the doors.

GEORGE PURCHASED FOUR belts, fastened each to the other, and threaded them between his mattress and box springs. Each night he brought the ends together and buckled himself beneath his quilts.

Years passed in this way, with George awaking early every morning strapped to his bed. His wife began sleeping across the hall and, when they stayed in motels, made him reserve nonadjoining rooms.

Visitors seldom came, but when they did, Sadie would take them on a tour of their home. By then every surface in the house—sideboard, dining and coffee table, ottoman, divan—was covered in antique glass. Sadie had acquired the largest collection in Perser and was slowly overtaking Herbert Nasser and his wife, Vinita, who made claim of the largest in Oklahoma.

Her guests would follow her through the small,

dark house, through the smell of must and old wood. There were two bedrooms, a bath, a small kitchen crowded with dining table and stove. None of the window blinds or curtains were open; Sadie feared those passing on the sidewalk would see inside. The worth of her collection was estimated at thirty thousand dollars.

"This piece is very old," she would tell her visitors, pointing to a candy dish. "I found it in a filling station outside Shreveport."

They nodded, ran their hands along its rim.

"And this piece," Sadie said, "I didn't think the man would part with it."

They nodded again, looked to their watches.

She would conclude her tour by showing George's room, the straps on his bed. The guests looked at her husband. They wanted to know how long it had been, if he would mind telling the story of his fall.

He would tell it. He knew it by rote: the platform, the derrick, the hospital, the dreams. It took him only fifteen minutes.

When he finished, his audience shook their heads. Often they reached to squeeze his hand or touch him on the arm. Sometimes they turned to Sadie and forced a smile.

She smiled back, gestured to George.

"This is what I have to live with," she would tell them.

• • •

IT WAS THEN 1957, the year Oral Roberts took a tent across the Midwest, bringing his revival to the lost and infirm. Sadie heard on the radio testimonies of those treated by Roberts. Some who had never walked made claim to walk. Some who had never seen claimed to see. Sharon Stilman was carried into his tent on a sheet and soon thereafter began a ministry of her own.

Sadie told her husband of this, and they drove 120 miles to a small town outside Tulsa, where for the past week Roberts had held a tent revival. They arrived late and sat toward the back.

George found much of the service consonant with what he had known from his childhood. There was a low stage and a choir on it, men in folding chairs dressed in ties and slacks and white shirts. There were rows of similar chairs for the audience, stapled pages containing a few hymns, sawdust on the floor, carpets down the aisles. Midway through, paper buckets with crosses stenciled on them were passed for offering.

After Roberts delivered a brief sermon, he asked those in need of healing to form a line to the left of the stage. He told them it did not have to be physical healing.

"There are three kinds of healing," he told them. "There is physical healing and emotional healing and healing of the spirit." He said God could perform all three.

Sadie leaned over, whispered to George. He shook his head. When she went to lean again, he rose from his seat and stepped in line.

Roberts sat at the edge of the stage with a handkerchief in one hand and a bottle of olive oil in the other. He was a young man: long nose, a long, smooth face. His hair was combed with tonic and laid back on his head. He wore a plain white shirt, a tie, gray slacks, polished black shoes. Between his legs stood a microphone tilted toward his mouth, positioned low on its stand.

Folks came and stood in front the stage, handed one of Roberts's assistants an index card on which was written their names and the names of their afflictions. These in turn were handed to Roberts.

George examined the blank card and the pencil he had been passed moments before. He looked to the evangelist who was addressing an elderly woman with braces on her legs.

"How long have you had this, sister?"

"I been this way since I was twenty-two," the woman told him.

Roberts dabbed oil into the palm of one hand and told her to come close. He leaned over the edge of the stage, put the hand to her cheek, and lifted the other toward the ceiling, praying into the microphone.

"Lord," he prayed, "deliver her."

The woman began to shiver; then her body became

rigid and she fell backward to the ground. A man in a dark suit came and covered her legs with a blanket. Another member of the audience approached, handed up her card. George watched all this, feeling of a sudden as if someone had hollowed him.

He started to turn, but just then one of Roberts's assistants happened down the line. He noticed George's card was blank and touched him on the elbow, inquiring after his affliction.

George shook his head, tried to step around the man, but found himself blocked by a row of card tables piled with books and pamphlets.

The man looked askance, leaned toward him, and George quickly told the story of his fall. When he finished, the other's face had an amazed look. He took George by the arm, parted the crowd, and led him onto the stage. They stood to the side while Roberts prayed, and then the man went to the evangelist and whispered into his ear.

Roberts turned. He rose, took the microphone from its stand, and walked to George. The crowd quieted. Roberts's voice in the microphone was wet and very loud.

"Tell these people your name."

George shifted from one foot to the other. He brought a hand from behind his back and scratched at his nose. "George Crider," he said.

"And you had an accident?" Roberts asked.

"Yes."

"You fell?"

"Yes."

"How far?"

"One hundred sixteen feet."

Many in the crowd gasped; some called to God.

"And you were hurt?"

"Yes."

"How many bones did you break?"

"All of them," George said.

The preacher put his hand on George's shoulder. "And what did the doctors say?"

George paused, looked down. "They told me I would never walk again."

There were a few moments of silence. Then the crowd began to stir and then to applaud. They cried in loud voices, and most all raised their hands. One man left his seat and began to run the aisles.

Roberts turned to face them. "Do you hear that?" he said. "The God that did this can do the same for you. The same God who caused this brother to walk after breaking every bone in his body can grant you your deliverance."

More folk left their seats and stepped in line. The preacher stood above them like an auctioneer.

George was led from the stage. He saw Sadie waiting for him near the ramp.

As he was about to walk away, the man who had discovered him asked if he would return the next night to give his testimony. George shook his head, took his wife by the arm, and escorted her from the tent.

IT WAS MORE than twenty years before he would visit another faith healer. By then George had retired from his job and begun to collect his pension. He and Sadie traveled most the year, attending antique shows, conventions, fairs and galleries. They acquired piece after piece, and in the 1969 edition of *Carnival Glass Anthology,* there was a black-and-white photo of his wife standing next to a bookcase full of depression-era teacups.

But, however great Sadie's satisfaction, George's condition grew worse. His hands would often shake and occasionally his vision blur. The man slept only two or three hours a night, and at times would go days on no sleep at all, walking through his afternoons with a glazed look. He did not talk about the dreams or the ailments that made him unfamiliar to his body. He refused to go back to the doctors or turn to the God of his father. He refused to take the shotgun from under the seat of the car and place the barrel in his mouth. Regardless, he found himself polishing the weapon once or twice a month, breaking it over at the dining-room table to check the shells.

In Denton, Texas, one night, Sadie forced him into a revival meeting held by the Reverend R. T. Shorbach. She told George that life with him had caused her to need healing of the spirit. George watched his wife leave her seat, walk the aisle, and take her place at the end of Shorbach's prayer line. He retrieved a hymnal from beside his chair and began to flip the pages.

Shorbach was an older gentleman from Tyler, Texas, who clothed his body in immense black suits. He had fat features and a welcoming face, thick eyebrows, a sweep of gray hair. The preacher smelled of strong cologne and sweat.

He stood down from the platform with a microphone, laying hands on those who came through his line. In front of each, he would pray loudly, examining the ceiling as people fell away from his thick fingers to the arms of an assistant.

After a while, George could no longer watch. He walked to the lobby, found a rest room and then a vending machine. He put quarters in, but the candy caught in a loop of the wire that held it. When he came back to the auditorium, his wife stood before the massive preacher. George crossed his arms and watched from the wings.

His wife seemed small from the distance. She was a petite woman still, her silver hair pinned in an elaborate bun. George watched as Shorbach's hand came to her forehead, watched Sadie's arms rise. He continued watching as her body went suddenly rigid and she fell backward into the arms of Shorbach's assistant. She was laid on the ground, covered with a blanket.

"Slain," Shorbach said over the swell of the organ, "slain in the Spirit."

The next night Sadie persuaded George to return to Shorbach's meeting, where she again approached the prayer line and soon lay sprawled on the floor.

A month later, in Biloxi, Mississippi, George would watch his wife fall from the hands of the Reverend Shorbach, and two months later in Little Rock, and six later in Atlanta. Sadie began keeping two schedules on her refrigerator, one of antique conventions, one of Shorbach's camp meetings. And several years later, when Sadie stepped from the prayer line in front of the man of God, he held the microphone away from his face and asked where he knew her from.

Sadie smiled, raised both hands, and braced herself for the fall.

YEARS PASSED. Numb years of sickness and pain. Sadie continued seeing Shorbach when the preacher came within driving distance of Perser. If George was too ill to take her, Sadie would phone a nephew to do so, and when he could not oblige, the woman closed the door to her bedroom and watched the broadcast on TBN.

In the past, George had been a quiet man; now he was utterly silent. He did not answer his wife's questions, and when visitors called, he would retreat to his work shed behind the house. He was in consid-

erable pain but took nothing for it. His lower back
had deteriorated, his shoulders and hips. Some morn-
ings it would take him upward of an hour to rise
from bed. The dreams, as ever, continued to shake
him, and he spent much time weighing the benefits
of life and death.

Then one evening, Sadie fell from the back porch.
She was putting out bread for squirrels, and she
slipped, snapping her leg below the knee. From the
shed, George heard his wife's screaming. He managed to position her in the backseat of the car, drive
her to the hospital. When they sent her home with a
cast and crutches, it was George who helped her to
bathe, brought her meals, took her from place to
place.

"George," Sadie would say. "I need to go."

George would trundle in, assist her to the bathroom, stand outside the door waiting.

It was late that summer when the First Pentecostal
brought in Leslie Snodgrass, an evangelist of fifteen,
already known across Oklahoma and much of Missouri. People said amazing things of the boy. They
claimed signs and wonders, miracles and healing and
salvation of the lost. He preached repentance, prayed
over the hopelessly ill. The young man came from a
small town outside Tishomingo and had been preaching since the age of six. He was short and fair, very
thin, but his voice was that of a man three times his
years, and audiences watched him with an amazed

look. The elders in the crowd would shout and sing, and sinners sat with whitened faces, sinking quietly in their seats. When Snodgrass ended his sermons, old and young alike would fall into the altars to seek mercy. He knelt among them and, when moved, stood to his feet and walked about, laying hands on the sick and troubled of spirit.

Sadie soon heard of this and began asking George to take her to one of these meetings. She wanted to see her leg heal quickly.

George had decided some time before he could not endure another service; he told his wife to find someone else. But Sadie was persistent, and in a matter of nights George found himself sitting along the rear wall of the church, listening to the young evangelist's words.

He watched with an expression no less amazed than those around him. It was indeed a sight to astonish. The boy moved like one possessed, his eyes tightly shut, wads of tissue clenched in his fists. There were hard men who had heard him preach and could not return to their former lives, but by this point George believed only in anguish, for that, he felt, was the truth of the world, and though entranced by the young man pacing the platform above him, he did not recover his faith.

The boy's sermon ended with an altar call, and the altars were soon full. George sat with open eyes, staring over the bowed heads. People knelt, wrestling with their spirits. Occasionally, an elder among them would raise his voice in travail. All prayed for what seemed a very long time, and then Snodgrass rose, approached the platform, and asked those in need of healing to come forward. Sadie began tugging at George's sleeve, wanting him to help her there.

George pulled her to her feet, positioned the crutches beneath her arms. She hobbled out into the aisle and began inching toward the altar, her husband following a few steps behind. They reached the row of people standing along the front of the sanctuary, found themselves a place at the far right. George made sure of Sadie, then leaned against the wall to take the weight from his back.

He watched Snodgrass make his way down the line. The boy had no microphone, no handkerchief or oil. He would stop and speak quietly with each, bow his head and whisper, sometimes laying a pale hand to the person's shoulder, his demeanor one of tranquillity, calm.

George was shocked to see the people remain standing. They did not fall; they did not quake or run the aisles. They stood their places with broken looks, the wise looks of the condemned.

George noticed his wife was also watching the boy, but her face held a bitter expression, more so the closer Snodgrass came. She seemed to understand that the evangelist would not lay hands to her forehead. He would not send her to the carpet, and no assistant would stand waiting with arms and a blanket. Sadie would leave just as she came, and realizing this, George began to chuckle quietly.

The boy came closer and Sadie's face grew harsher, and as Snodgrass was praying for the man next to her, she spun suddenly from the line, casting George derision as she turned.

George watched his wife go up the aisle, past the pew where they'd formerly sat, out the double doors into the lobby. A louder laugh escaped his lips, and when he turned back around, his face was cracked from smiling. Snodgrass stood in front of him.

George's laughter died, and he watched the evangelist with an anxious look, failing for a moment to blink or breathe. The boy was utterly ashen, and he walked sternly up, raised his hand, and placed it to the old man's chest, closing his eyes to mumble a few words. George did not catch them. Only, the moment they left the boy's lips, the audience beheld George Crider fall like lightning.

It did not seem so to George. To him his descent seemed to take a very long time. At first there was the feeling his legs had given way, his limbs wilted to nothing. He sensed his arm go numb and a terrific burst go off in his chest just to the left of where the boy had touched him. He felt warm there and very still and the air that buzzed about his ears was like fire.

There was time for George to consider many things

before he struck the ground, to consider a time before dreams troubled his sleep, before an injury placed him in a hospital bed. He considered walking forty miles through the Quashita forest, under the pines and cedars of southeast Oklahoma, and then the time of his boyhood under the dense trees, before his brother had fallen, before he had a brother at all. He considered when it was only he and his mother and his father, when they would pick him off the ground, only a child of four years then, place him in the center of a patchwork quilt, and lift him, allowing him to leave the fabric for a moment before he sank back to its folds. They repeated this for what seemed like hours—though it could not have been so long—the thin child rising and falling, caught up, snapped into the air.

It was weightless, that sense, the stomach a rush, face and arms and legs prickling, the heart feeling as if it might split. Rising and falling, and again, and over. If it had always been like that, there would have been point in nothing else but to live in the instant when gravity first took hold and pulled you to its center.

George considered this of all things as he abandoned himself to the fall, unaware he would expire some sixteen inches above the carpet, that his body would strike the floor with a hollow sound.

COURTSHIP

―――――

For every female who makes
herself male will enter heaven's kingdom.
— THE GOSPEL OF THOMAS

JANSEN WOULD NOT believe *gay* the right word for
it. In high school he courted several women and
liked it just fine, the way they looked and touched
him. He did not act in a manner you'd think queer,
didn't stare at other men or grow excited when he
saw one on TV. He'd decided that his yearnings for
Wisnat were not, by definition, homosexual, for
surely this label treated of appetites universally, not
cases specific. There had to be another term, a word
not yet invented. The bartender spent his days pon-
dering this, for it mattered to him greatly what things
were called. The issue, he began to think, was less
about male and female and more about feeling—the
emotions divorced from gender. Unfortunately, in
his case this feeling was strong: heart drooping to-

ward stomach, head buzzing, bowels in a clench. Often, his tongue held a steeled taste at its tip and his eyes jerked nervously about. After much deliberation, many soul-searched nights polishing his length of counter (dictionary lying dog-eared just beneath the register), Jansen concluded he was not gay at all. He concluded his sexual proclivities were straight as the next man's and the emotional maelstrom he weathered about one thing alone — love.

Dennison Wisnat was the vortex of this storm. Jansen could remember sitting across from him at Sunday school (plastic veneer table, coloring books of apostles, Pentecostal matron with her hair woven into a great gray bun). He was barely ten, but there was already something about the brows of the boy that drew him. They were not, as are those of the average child, smooth arcs; nor were they the circumflexed ridges of children more starkly handsome. Wisnat's eyebrows ran level across their tops, falling sharply at their ends toward the crow's-feet that would appear in later decades. The effect of this was to give his face a solemn cast, to make the boy appear dejected and, in Jansen's view, wizened by that dejection. He didn't know quite what he wanted to do with Wisnat's features, whether sculpt or pencil them into a sketchbook, mold a thin facsimilar mask and wear it atop his own. He shook away such thoughts (others more disturbing riding, inevitably, their heels), telling himself, at any rate, that such was the relationship of Peter and the Lord, such the rapport of anyone worth the title of friend.

But regardless of pretext, it was there that the bartender's love began, directed toward his playmate and fellow parishioner, festering over the years to come. Wisnat and Jansen grew inseparable, the latter failing to understand his feelings (little enough confess them), the former gathering every attractive woman that steered along his path. Wisnat was not a high school athlete but managed to accomplish his goals otherwise, keeping at bay the impending darkness through relations with the opposite sex.

Small-town idyll: the drive-in in midsummer, large screen flickering, speaker balanced on half-rolled window, two couples amorous, oblivious of whereabouts. Wisnat is behind the steering wheel, grown to well over six feet, seventeen years of age, thick haired and muscular. The young lady (two years his senior) sits almost in his lap. She gropes and caresses, acts on him, he the disinterested watcher of this play, hands loosely on her back, sad eyes open, reflecting the scene. He seems not to be mindful— she no more to him than an item in a series and, *after all*, thinks Jansen, *is he any more to her?* Wisnat looks forward to the next, past the robotic arms and pulleys, down the assembly line, and seeing them extend into the hazed horizon, his eyes are a little less sad—the dream of one to whom he will be more than just an achievement, whose survival will depend on him, this illumines the darkness, makes it bearable. *Perhaps for a moment,* muses Jansen, who in the backseat is likewise engaged. Jansen peers over the shoulder of his date and into the rearview mirror to see Wisnat's strange expression (open-eyed, unfocused, fogged by dream), watching his friend carefully, praying that the girl he is kissing does not open her painted eyes.

THEN THE COLLEGE years. University of Oklahoma. Jansen majoring in hotel management, Wisnat in business. They lived together in an apartment complex: single bedroom with bath and kitchen, balcony overlooking the division's pool. Summer and spring, Wisnat held forth from this gallery, occasionally settling his beer in his lap to wave up the women who would be sunbathing below, waiting, it seemed to Jansen, only for invitation. He would open the door and lead them out to Wisnat—brows drooping at the sides of his sunglasses—then go back and sit in his recliner to observe. Sometimes the newly introduced couple would make their way back through the sliding glass doors, across the carpet, down the hall to the bedroom. Jansen registered every moan of mouth and squeak of springs, calmly recorded them, smiling. He would match eyes with Wisnat when he emerged, an inquisitive look on his face yet hardly one of annoyance.

Though one might have thought these trysts would

make Jansen writhe with jealousy or, at the very least be reluctant to assist with his friend's seductions, the converse was true. Jansen misjudged Wisnat's desire as he misjudged his own (even then the belief that he was homosexual plagued him, and he would push it away with flawed syllogisms: *I am not gay, gays are interested in sex. I am only in love*). He envisioned Wisnat's libido a pit, not bottomless but very large. When that pit was full (the quicker it was full), Jansen thought he might profess his feelings and be met with something other than a blank stare or fist. As he led each woman onto the balcony, Jansen pictured a pile of female bodies slowly rising, torso by torso, ineluctably filling the chasm in Wisnat's cratered soul.

A month into his junior year (the pit's bottom, he'd decided, was beginning to come into sight), Jansen's father died. Six months later, his mother followed. He stood above her grave with Wisnat's hand on his shoulder (the young man's eyes still sadder than those of his mourning friend), thumbing, in his pocket, the insurance check he'd just been handed. They made the hour's drive from Perser back to Norman: silence, whirring of tires on imperfect stretches of pavement, more silence. Back in their apartment, Jansen went into the bathroom and, cupping water to his face, found several strands of black hair wound around the stopper. He unspooled them, checked them against his own, turned on the overhead light and began to examine his scalp. Though his hair was relatively thick, though he had just come from the funeral of his mother, an additional worry began to shudder through him. The grief of loved ones gone and the anxiety over love uncaptured appeared to be taking its toll.

Over the next year he found the same black hairs along the floor in the bedroom, on the kitchen stove, along the back of the recliner. Squatting one day, naked and wet, he pulled an enormous clump of them from the drain in the shower. He conducted rigorous inspections of his scalp and could see no patches, but he knew it was only a matter of time before they began to show. He could not guess how Wisnat might feel about this, wondered if this alone would prevent their union. As if in sympathy Wisnat brought no more women into the apartment, his expression beyond sadness now, nearing apocalypse.

And then there was the day Jansen was doing laundry, stooped to the dryer, and found a dried ball of black hair spinning in the whites: a tumbleweed among the T-shirts and sheets. Clutching it in a fist, he went upstairs and walked out to the balcony to confess his affliction. The sun was setting, dyeing the world in crimson. Jansen steered his eyes away, feeling, of a sudden, very old. He approached Wisnat from behind, laid a hand to his shoulder and, looking down, saw an almost bare patch on the crown of the seated man's head.

"Jansen," Wisnat told him, without turning, without raising his voice above a whisper, "I think I'm going bald."

THE WOMEN STOPPED. Just that quickly, it was over. The balcony doors were shut and the blinds drawn across them. Jansen watched his friend in the wavering light of the television, watched him shed hair after hair until all that was left was a furred ridge running atop his ears and winding about the base of his skull. He did not know it was possible for one to grow bald so quickly and continued to check his own hair for fear the same might happen to him. But part and tug as he might (bent across the sink with a comb in one hand, a tuft of hair in the other), Jansen looked much as he always had. If anything, his hair had become thicker.

That fall, Wisnat withdrew from the business program and enrolled in beautician's school. He didn't discuss the decision, did not remark at any time afterward. Jansen came into the living room one evening and saw Wisnat had replaced a *Cost Accounting* textbook with one that detailed the procedures for and innovations in hair dye. He could not confront Wisnat. A new emotion seemed to be bleeding the cracks of his friend's sad mask, one of complete and utter desperation. Jansen knew Wisnat was not interested in the field, didn't care about haircuts, hair products, the proper way to give a perm. He knew the way Wisnat's mind operated—calculating, machinelike, the logic of the assembly line dictating his ethics and morale. His friend, propped in the recliner with a hundred-page study of testosterone, was searching for a way to regrow hair.

For hours each day, Wisnat would explore his options—on the Internet, in the library, faxes coming from e-mail contacts through a local Kinko's. He attempted every remedy he could discover: herbal or folkloric, pharmaceutical or electronic. There were pills and tonics; scalp massages and conditioners; oils, applicators, liquid vitamins; an expensive cap that plugged into the wall. He scoured medical journals and health books, ancient tomes revealing therapies by peoples now extinct. Using Jansen's student ID, he registered for a chemistry course that met evenings, learning just enough to inform his doctors why their treatments were unsuccessful. Arms crossed to their chests, they would shake their heads, reminding Wisnat who held a degree in medicine, who was earning a beautician's. The patient returned their looks, unblinking.

Upon their respective graduations, Jansen and Wisnat loaded their belongings into a U-Haul and moved into the deserted house of the former's deceased parents, back outside the oil town of Perser. Jansen used the insurance money that had been accruing interest to purchase an isolated, rural bar, one mile south of the Pentecostal church. After renovations and six months' business, he bought also a barbershop that had recently come up for sale, signing the deed over to Wisnat. (The man was now acquiring a belly to accompany his balding skull. Though Jansen's love for him had not faltered, he hated to see Wisnat metamorphose into something so pale, so hairless and bloated. The desperation had faded from Wisnat's face only to be replaced by an even more profound expression, one redolent of despair.) Jansen walked in, pitched him the keys, and as if that action had triggered an engine, Wisnat woke the next morning and dressed in his barber's smock and slacks. He drove down Main Street, pulled in front of his new shop, unlocked the doors, turned the OPEN sign streetward, without pause pressing a button that started the red-and-white pole spinning in its cylinder of glass, this candy cane signaling to the barber neither pleasure nor sweetness but rather an attendant decay.

AND SO THEY entered a new era, a period so like marriage that the two refused to make jokes about it. Not because it did not occur to them to do so but rather because the obviousness of such comedy would have killed the laughter before it left their throats.

The bar Jansen purchased established a faithful

clientele (mindful of his town's history, he named it the Gusher), one that expanded with each new week. He would awaken late in the morning, dither about the house in his robe, drive into town to meet Wisnat for lunch. They'd walk across the street to a shop that sold coffee and sandwiches, Jansen carrying the conversation, Wisnat responding with an occasional nod. Wisnat had never been one to ramble, rationing his speech as a stranded man does water. Now he seemed all but mute. Perhaps, Jansen tried to convince himself, the customers were wearing on him— making small talk about weather and mortgages and farm equipment for eight hours a day was affecting his desire to speak. But behind his self-delusions, Jansen knew Wisnat had traversed some desert of the mind, a pair of footprints tracking an infinity of sand. His friend, as he'd known him, might not be coming back.

Late in the night when both men were in their rooms, Jansen would lie awake listening to crickets outside his window, the hum of the refrigerator, the house settling. He imagined he could hear Wisnat from across the hall, the rhythmic noises of inhalation, the serene breathing of the unconscious. Often, he would climb out of bed, move the door on its hinges, creep the expanse of hallway, and peer into the near blackness of Wisnat's room—moonlight framing the blackout shades, the face of a glow-in-the-dark clock. He thought many times about making his way farther, to his friend's bed, parting the covers and sheets, sliding in between. But what, he began to ask himself, would he encounter once he reached the warm body in its center? What would be left to embrace?

The more time that passed, the more Jansen did not want to answer such questions. It was no longer a fear of being met with outrage (*What are you doing, Jansen? What the hell do you think you're . . .*); these were issues he'd assuaged in 1,001 nighttime fantasies: explanations and reasoning, a long silence wherein enlightenment might take sudden hold. What troubled Jansen was the fact that even if he were able to negotiate the minefield of Wisnat's confusion, even if able to settle his friend's nerves and allay his panic, he would be faced with nothing but a shell, a hollow parody of the man he had known. For almost a year, Wisnat had been an automaton, his emotions gone beneath the surface, his desire extinguished. How could he recognize love, much less return it?

So, standing at the door, Jansen bided his time, hoping for that thing inside Wisnat to regain its consciousness, for the sleeper to awake. He stared into the darkened room and waited for those eyes to lose their blank and mechanical hopelessness, to become, once again, merely sad.

• • •

It was a Thursday night when Megan made her first appearance, ladies' night at the Gusher. Jim Peters, an overweight veteran, foreman on a legion of the town's construction jobs, had been playing the video trivia machine Jansen installed a week earlier, sliding quarters in the slot and mumbling, his broad face narrowed, scrunched to the screen.

"Vanna White?" he was whispering to himself. Turning to Wade Stevenson—a thin man, thoroughly defeated, Laurel to his companion's Hardy—he rocked drunkenly on his stool. "Fuck's Vanna White?"

Wade looked frailly over. "Game show," the man explained. "Turns the letters."

"Miss America?" Peters asked.

"Huh?"

"She the Miss America was in *Hustler*?"

"Naw," Wade said, snapping his fingers, "that's what's her face—"

"Williams," Jansen told them.

"That's right," said Wade, "Vanna Williams."

"Vanessa," Jansen corrected.

"Vanessa Williams."

Peters looked back to the screen, pressed a neon button. A red *X* reflected off his glasses.

"Shit," he said.

For most the evening, Jansen had been wiping the south end of the counter, glancing occasionally at Wisnat, who for the first night in weeks had decided to come to the bar for drinks. He was by himself at the dartboard, making impassive throws, dislodging them from the cork, making them again. Over the last several months he had grown completely bald or, perhaps, after giving up his quest, had merely begun shaving what hair remained—Jansen was uncertain which. The bartender was looking directly at him when the front door opened and the room's acoustics shifted in pitch, jukebox country spilling into the foyer. It was for this reason that his first impression of the woman would not be the slight alteration in sound or even her actual image when he turned in a moment toward the entrance. Jansen's initial reaction would be forever filtered through Wisnat—the blurred likeness of the door reflected off his polished head, that head turning and its eyes coming about, giving a look Jansen had never before seen on the barber's face. It was neither sadness nor desperation, this look; certainly not the blank gaze that seemed, these days, to be permanently etched in his features. This, the bartender decided, was something else.

Jansen went to greet the woman making for the empty barstool beside Peters and Wade. Close to five nine, he calculated, five ten. She was wearing a midriff and jeans, and she looked tall in the heels she wore—she might have been six feet in the heels. Her stomach was flat and tan, and her navel was pierced with a bright silver ring, and this ring had another linked through it with a bell that jingled when she walked. She was blond, not a speck of makeup, with hair to her hips, and blue eyes—*otherworldly,* thought Jansen: small ears like an elf, small, soft, elfin features.

Peters, together with the rest of the men, watched her walk the floor, then hunkered between his shoulders, raised his glass, and muttered into his beer.

"They God Almighty," he said.

The woman drew back a stool, set her purse in its seat, began digging inside. She pulled out cigarettes, a lighter, a small brown leather wallet. As the bar registered her movements, Jansen put down his towel, walked over, and asked what she'd like. The response was a White Russian. The bartender nodded, took the vodka, Kahlúa, and cream from beneath the counter, poured them in equal portions into a glass, scooped in several ice cubes, settled the drink on a coaster between the woman's elbows.

"How much?" she asked.

"Three fifty," he told her.

She slid four singles across the counter, released a tranquil smile.

Seeing this, Wade and Peters scooted back their stools. "We'll see you," Peters said.

The bartender looked up, asked if they were leaving. It was only, he reminded them, a quarter till nine.

"We got to be out there to pour that concrete at six," Peters told him, wiping his mustache.

"We got to get," said Wade.

"Bossman don't pay us to be late, Jansen."

"We got to go," Wade said.

Jansen saw the All-Kraft Konstruction logo on Peters's shirt disappear out the door, took the woman's money to the register. As he fitted the bills into their cubbies, he located Wisnat between two bottles of scotch in the bar's mirror. The man was sitting beneath the dartboard, feigning interest in a hockey game on the television hung above the counter—glancing, on occasion, toward the woman. The blank expression was indeed gone. It seemed that the old sadness had awoken to replace it, but this sadness was compromised by that other something Jansen had noticed before, an anxiety, maybe—perhaps what passed with Wisnat for desire.

Then, suddenly, Jansen was unaware of himself. Something struck him with the force of a blow, the apprehension a runner receives when he is in front, only a few feet from the finish line, his opponents yards behind. As if the entire race had been free of worry precisely because he never let himself believe that winning was an option, didn't allow victory to distort his senses, cloud his mind. But now with the unbroken tape within grasp, what fantasies of failure will assail him: whether twist of ankle or sprain of knee or, possibly, disasters more far-fetched—environmental mishaps, nuclear war, the Rapture. For Jansen, turning, seeing the woman as if for the first time, no longer observes a person of beauty, a woman enjoying a drink, but sees rather a pit stacked nearly level, a place inside for one more body and, if properly positioned, if perfectly placed, the fulfillment of his dreams.

JANSEN RECLINES IN the barber's chair; Wisnat stands above him. The barber gathers foam from the palm of his cupped hand and dabbing it, spreads it across his client's face. He makes, almost, a mask of it, a cast of lathered white. Then it is out with his razor and its calm, smooth strokes—up the neck, over the cheeks, scrapes on the underside of Jansen's pointed nose. Tightly caped, the man closes his eyes and allows the barber to work on him, barely comprehending the syllables, the urgency in his companion's voice.

The topic is the woman from the previous night. He calls her simply "the girl," for they do not yet know her name. Wisnat has plans for her should she come in the bar again, wants to know if the bartender will help with these plans, wants to know the *odds* of her coming in.

The odds.

His opinion.

Jansen?

"Opinion of what?" says the bartender, having decided beforehand to play this coy.

"The girl," Wisnat tells him.

"She seemed nice," Jansen noncommits. "Very nice girl."

The shaving stops. When he opens his eyes, he sees Wisnat has crossed his arms, the razor passive against his smock, his expression strained-looking, severe. The bartender has not seen this side of his friend. It frightens him.

"I don't like my chances," says Wisnat.

"Chances of what?"

No answer.

"A date?"

Wisnat nods.

"I'm sure they're good. Why wouldn't they be good?"

The barber merely looks at him. Jansen brushes a spot of foam from his cheek. He points to one side of his face—the unshaven side.

"Are you going to—"

"I need an edge," Wisnat tells him.

"Edge?"

"Yes."

"What kind of edge?"

"Any," says the barber.

Jansen, about to rise and bolster his friend's esteem, is pushed gently back, the razor at work again, the sounds of soft scraping. He closes his eyes, then relaxes, imagines, for an instant, the woman. He pictures tucking her arms and legs, folding her into a large square. Then hefting this brick, fitting it snugly into place.

Evening, for the bartender, cannot get here too quickly.

IT WOULD HAVE been difficult to determine who was more pleased. For that night, when the woman arrived at the bar, there was a look of ardor on the faces of Wisnat and Jansen both.

She arrived, crossed to the counter, settled her purse into the selfsame seat. Jansen prepared her White Russian, starting a conversation in which the woman revealed more than the bartender had hoped. Her name was Megan Thomas (having a strong Southern accent, she drew the syllables out, pronouncing them May-gun), and she'd recently moved from Missouri to take a job at Perser Memorial Hospital. She was, by her own account, much younger than she looked, had a history of bad relationships, issues with self-respect. Since the move, she'd been desperate for company: on the phone every evening with her mother or aunt, friends back in the Ozarks. Jansen—in an attempt to stall Megan until he could summon his friend—began asking a series of questions to which the woman responded with sincerity and candor.

No, she'd not thought of a dating service.

No, she didn't read the personals.

No, regardless of how hard it was for him to believe it, she was rarely asked out. She had a way, she'd been told, of intimidating men.

As she spoke, Jansen nodded, trying to entice Wisnat over, to find a way of introducing the two. But Wisnat remained where he was, huddled beneath the dartboard drinking bourbon and Cokes, observing, from beneath his sloping brows, Jansen talking with the woman—this woman laughing, reaching to touch the bartender on the arm, spinning a straw in the corner of her mouth.

Indeed, Wisnat was all but silent on the matter until the next day when Jansen was back in the chair with the sheet draped across him, face smeared with shaving cream. But on this occasion, when Jansen opened his eyes he did not see Wisnat standing cross-armed and anxious but rather the barber's palm extended in front of his face, in its center several small tablets—orange and flat, shaped, Jansen would later think, like stop signs.

"You've got to cut them in half," began Wisnat, using an index finger to demonstrate the motion. "Cut them in half and crush them between a couple of spoons."

Jansen looked at the medication, then the barber.

"What are they?" he asked.

"They're pills."

"What are they *for?*"

"The girl," he was told. "You stir them in her drink. But first you have to crush them into powder."

"Wisnat—"

"You have turn them into dust."

"You're not serious."

The barber indicated he was.

"What do they do?"

Wisnat closed his fist around the tablets, sunk them into a pocket. He took up the razor and moved toward Jansen. The bartender pushed away his arm.

"Wisnat," he said, "what do they *do?*"

The barber took a step away, looked toward the street. His answer, when it came, made very little sense. Jansen asked again, was again told.

Rising in his chair, Jansen took off the cape. He stared at Wisnat, stood staring at this man he'd known for most his life. He shook his head and exited the barber's shop, went to the Gusher, the conversation still turning in his head. He very nearly laughed at it, at someone having asked him to do this. He could lose his license. His parents' life savings. He carried cases of liquor from the storeroom, walked them toward the counter, looking at the bar, *his* bar, all of it jeopardized by the mere entertainment of this idea. He would not do it. He would refuse Wisnat something so ludicrous. Who, after all, did he think he was? There were limits, the bartender decided, even to love.

And so it was, that evening, when Megan arrived, when the pills (already crushed) slid into her drink, Jansen continued to ponder that afternoon's conversation, as he stirred the powder and the vodka, the Kahlúa and the cream.

Wisnat, he would remember asking, *what do they do?*

His reply was simple enough, the type of answer one uses for delusion, a thorough washing of the hands.

They make women so you can talk to them.

THE CHOICES WE MAKE. The treacherous instant in which we see ourselves as characters in a story: the crucial decision, the moment of crisis. Everything, we begin to think, must follow from here. It cushions us, does it not? Makes us disbelieve the reality, the complexity with which we've engaged. Life, henceforth, will assume a tighter structure, move toward an inevitable denouement. There will be an ending we will stand apart from, observe with disinterest. All the clutter will be removed and we will be granted a brief vision into what we truly are. We will behold our very natures, unclouded and frozen, reflected all at once in God's eternal mirror.

This is what Jansen thought. Evening after evening he drove to his bar, out Highway 9 with the air conditioner running and the windows rolled down, past the First Pentecostal: the small church he'd grown up in, left at the age of sixteen and never returned. He thought that the church had added to this viewing of himself as a dramatic figure. It was something for Jansen to measure himself against, a means of adopting a position from outside and surveying his soul.

The church was in revival that summer: all the cars in neat rows on the white gravel, the stray family running behind schedule, the sign facing the highway. He remembered revivals quite vividly, the weeklong (sometimes monthlong) meetings wherein the parishioners would rededicate their lives to holiness. Evangelists with handkerchiefs and polyester suits would preach of fire and death, the book of Revelation, the judgments reserved for those who abused their bodies with cigarettes and alcohol, promiscuity and drugs, television, liberal politics, homosexuality, makeup, rock and roll—all liars and whoremongers, thieves and murderers, sinners and backslidden Christians caught up at the last day and cast into a lake of fire.

As a boy, the fear of such a place was on him. He hit adolescence, felt a desire denounced from the very pulpit, and the fear swelled, ruled his existence as a palpable force. He became a teenager, left the church, professed atheism, and the fear was on him stronger than ever. In the dead of night, Jansen pictured scenes more vibrant than even the preachers could create: regions of pit and ash, time's livid flames extending into days unmarked by torment. He rolled on his bed, confessed sins enacted and imagined, awakened in the morning to grainy dawn and a love he could seldom understand.

But it was also this love that in his first years of college anchored him, kept him from returning to his faith out of simple fear. As long as there was Wisnat, this physical entity walking about, he could push away thoughts of fantastic and eternal torture. He could focus entirely on his roommate, justify his yearnings with the one Christlike emotion agreed on by all denominations, charismatic or otherwise.

Now, as an adult of almost thirty, Jansen no longer feared Hell, no longer lay awake constructing mentally its antechambers and dungeons. But whenever he was quiet, whenever there was neither light nor sound to distract him, the residue of past threats would present itself as a nagging anxiety—the sense that something was not right, something somewhere unfixably and permanently wrong. And while Wisnat contributed to such feelings, he also, by his mere presence, allayed them. Even the desire Jansen felt for his friend had become something on which the bartender could depend. He could not afford to lose him.

This, more than anything else, was how Jansen in the years to come would justify putting the pills in Megan's drinks. He knew it was not right—every nerve in him screamed against it—but what choice did he have? What was he to do when the man with whom he was in love asked of him a favor—one that, after all, was probably harmless, probably, thought Jansen, would not even produce its intended effect. At worst, Wisnat would not get what he was seeking and things would return to the way they'd been. At best, this would be Wisnat's final conquest, the beginning of what Jansen had imagined since he was a boy of ten.

DAYS OF AVOIDING his housemate, immersing himself in dictionaries, copying passages from the *OED*. Nights of tending bar, monitoring Wisnat, making Megan her off–White Russians. He tracks the origin of words like *perfidy*. Grinds, between spoons, pill after pill.

Weeks of such activity bled together. Jansen watched each evening for the drug to take effect, saw nothing but a rash on the woman's cheeks. Though he had hoped for Wisnat's quick success, Jansen soon grew so troubled that he immediately wished the entire business done. At first, he feared the pills might be Rohypnol, known in the media as the date-rape drug. But Rohypnol, Jansen learned, had an immediate effect, and whatever he was giving this woman didn't seem to be working at all, unless the goal was merely to chap her face. Perhaps, he figured, Wisnat had purchased some kind of aphrodisiac, answered an ad in the back of *Rolling*

Stone. Having flirted with similar ideas himself, Jansen knew that, whatever their promises, these pills were worthless.

He had begun to grow accustomed to Megan. For the first time, the bartender could entertain the possibilities of having a woman as a friend. It was obvious that she had developed a minor crush— *perfectly innocent,* thought Jansen, *completely natural.* It was also clear to him that even if Wisnat had permitted, he could hardly have returned her feelings. While he enjoyed speaking with her—thought her amusing and sincere—sexually, his reactions were of indifference. And, as if sensitive to his response, the woman, it seemed to Jansen, began to withdraw.

She continued, regardless, to frequent the Gusher. For weeks, she was faithful as ever. But the insecurities Megan had confessed seemed gradually to deepen, her confidence to steadily deflate. The bartender supposed this was a function of his refusing to promote her advances, but then he knew differently. Megan had developed the look of one wrestling with something, her expression going from shock, to frustration, to distress. He had seen the same progression in Wisnat when the man began losing his hair.

It was not worth it, Jansen finally concluded; it simply wasn't right. He had poured the entire bottle of pills down the sink when she abruptly quit coming.

Jansen did not have time to question her disappearance, for immediately his attention was focused on Wisnat. From the time the pills began going into Megan's drinks, Wisnat's unease had been apparent. He sat, no longer passive, beneath the dartboard, bouncing his knees, drinking bourbon, staring expectantly at the woman, his eyebrows slanting more solemnly that ever. She'd seemed not to notice him, this man leaning forward in his chair as if toward a film whose climax had arrived. Jansen had looked at Wisnat, incapable of comprehending his strategy. Why didn't he try and talk to her? For what, wondered Jansen, was he waiting?

When Megan quit coming to the bar, Wisnat's anxiety seemed to double. Unable now to study the woman, he sat at the counter observing the door, checking his watch, asking the bartender once more about the odds of her coming in. Jansen claimed not to know. He was disgusted with Wisnat, disgusted with himself. He despised the situation thoroughly, the part he'd played in it. Most of all he hated that after the fiasco was at an end, his emotions compelled him to reassure a man who was by all accounts a criminal.

There were nights when Wisnat would sit and stare at the entrance, and nights when he would interrogate Jansen, and nights when both men would begin drinking and be forced to have a cab conduct them home. Nights of narrowly averted arguments and migraine headaches and silences that would last for hours at a stretch. And finally there was the night (the beginning in Perser of Derrick Days, the town's annual celebration of its oil boom) when Jansen emerged from the storeroom into a packed house and saw that Megan had returned, that she was sitting, not in her usual spot, but as far from the counter as possible, by herself at a shadowed table; and walking toward her he saw for the first time that she was wearing makeup, and not just a light foundation or brush of rouge but a heavy covering agent intended to hide the most serious blemishes; and when he came closer, when the crowd parted and the light from the MILLER GENUINE sign illumined her face, Jansen saw, at long last, the effects of Wisnat's pills, saw on this woman's face, where the makeup was thickest, the shadow cast on her upper lip, not by her nose or the various objects depending from the walls (neon signs and lamps, the rack holding eleven damaged cues) but rather by a blond and slightly velveteen mustache.

THERE WAS BARELY room to stand and the noise was deafening, customers lined for much of the night, around the counter, obscure gestures signaling their choices of drink. Derrick Days was a popular event, known among the residents of towns throughout central Oklahoma. For years the Gusher had figured as one of its most prominent attractions. As soon as the first hint of summer dusk descended, people drove out in search of alcohol. They came in from firework shows, from the community center, from Parson's Field where the tractor pull was held. Their cars choked the parking lot, contending, in spectacle, with the revival not a mile down the road.

All that evening Jim Peters had been taunting the young man Jansen hired to help him on busier occasions, a red-haired college student by the name of Sparks. Peters took it as an affront that there should be someone of Sparks's age who had aspirations toward higher ed, and the drunker he became the more stabbing were his insults.

"What you need to go to college for anyway?" he was asking Sparks. "Cain't you already count?"

Wade, from a few stools over, ejected a snort. "Maybe he wants to be president."

"Shit," Peters told him, "he don't need college for that."

Sparks continued wiping at the counter. "You guys are real comedians," he said.

"Well, I'm glad you think so," Peters responded. Reaching across the counter, he put an enormous hand into Sparks's hair, mussed it.

Sparks retreated, realigned, with his fingers, the part. "Quit it," he warned.

Jansen, not wanting to deal with a brawl, asked

Sparks to help him pull several cases of vodka from the back. The two of them walked toward the storeroom, the bartender cautioning the young man about getting into a scuffle with the larger and more aggressive veteran.

Emerging, Jansen carried a box of liquor toward the counter and noticed Megan at her table. He'd started toward her across the bar—skirting tables, dodging clusters of drunks—reached a certain point, and then, stopping in midstep, registered with horror, the mustache, the results of the barber's enterprise. It flooded in on him, the entirety of Wisnat's plan. For several moments, he did not breathe.

Abruptly, a stranger at a nearby table gave a tug on Jansen's sleeve. "I think your buddy's in trouble," said his voice. Glancing behind him, shaken from his thoughts, Jansen saw that a case of vodka lay broken on the floor. There was a large commotion and then a ring of men, two figures struggling in its center. Between a pair of upraised and riotous arms, Jansen watched Peters twirl Sparks and twist him into a half nelson.

"Come on," the man was saying, veins articulating along the insides of his arms, "give us a hug."

"Yeah," said Wade, "give him a hug."

The bartender rushed over, helped loosen Peters's grip, asked the man to let Sparks go. Peters went gradually slack and then released his captive alto-

48

gether. Jansen conducted him swiftly from the ring, cries of disappointment general in the room.

"Aw," begged Peters, "don't take my little Sparkie away."

Shaking his head, Jansen brought Sparks behind the counter, tried to calm him. The boy slung a towel spectacularly at the bar, cast Peters an indignant look. "Fat fuck," he said, under his breath.

Jansen glanced quickly toward Megan's table, noticing that Wisnat—the man had been invisible up till then; the bartender was not even aware of his attendance—was standing there talking to her. Megan was nodding.

"What's that?" said Peters, interrupting Jansen's attempts to project his hearing. He rose, again, to his feet, swayed back and forth. "What'd you say?"

Sparks stood for a moment. Jansen tried to draw him back to the storeroom, but the boy maneuvered out of the bartender's grip. From the corner of his eye he saw Wisnat pull back a chair, sit down next to Megan.

Sparks leaned over the bar, brought his face against Peters's. "Fat fucking fuck," he slowly enunciated, spraying spit across the veteran's glasses.

Peters threw back his head and began laughing, Jansen exhaling in relief. Then Peters grabbed Sparks, drug him over the counter, and tossed him in the floor, wedging both knees in the young man's chest.

"Get off me," came the muffled voice of Sparks. "The fuck off me."

Peters unbuckled his belt and began to lower his pants. "This fat man's going to shit right in your skinny, little face," he said.

It took four men to lift Peters off Sparks. When they seated him in his stool he sat there pointing at the boy, laughing. "You're a lucky son of a bitch," he informed the bar. "I judged the chili cook-off this afternoon."

Laughter. The mock screams of women.

Jansen, untucking the front of his shirt to mop at his face, asked Wade to call a cab. It arrived almost instantly, Peters asleep the moment he was crammed inside. When Jansen walked back into the bar and began searching around, he saw that Megan was gone. The barber as well.

Locating Sparks, he asked where he went.

"Where *who* went?" The boy was standing behind the counter with an icepack on his forehead, a look in his eyes of rage and relief.

"Wisnat," repeated Jansen, "where is he?"

"Left," Sparks told him, motioning to the rear exit. He sat the icepack on the bar and miniature streams of water ran toward its edge. "Went out the back with some bimbo."

IT WAS AFTER two when the last of them stumbled out, lights from a dozen cars fanning, at various angles, the bar's rear wall. Walking to the center of the room, Jansen collapsed into a chair. All of the windows facing the highway were smeared with fingerprints, and there was a word greased on the outside pane that he could not make out. He sat for some time, attempting to decipher it, feeling, of a sudden, as if he were going to be ill.

Rising, he began to busy himself with cleaning the room. There were crushed beer nuts strewn across the floor and ashtrays brimming with half-smoked cigarettes, matchbooks laid out in ominous patterns, arranged by an anonymous seer. On one of the tables someone had constructed a miniature castle out of straws and Michelob bottles. The bartender left this fortress intact, picked up the larger items and washed the dishes, swept the floors and wiped the countertop. He went behind the bar, ejected the register's tray, tallied the currency into careful stacks, zipped all of it into a First National bag. Glancing into the mirror, he saw a pair of lights strobe the roadside windows, come glaring up, cut to darkness. He heard a car door slam, the front door open. Tossing the bank bag beneath the counter, he turned. Wisnat stood before him, his face bled of the hopelessness and anxiety that had been so long engraved there, his brows not even reverting to their familiar, dissatisfied slope. There was a new expression on the man's face, one, it almost seemed, of contentment. He walked to where Jansen had been sitting and pulled back a chair.

As Jansen had cleaned the bar, he'd contemplated how he would approach the man, what he might say. Numerous insults and chastisements ran through his mind, each more severe than the one before. Now, with Wisnat seated barely fifteen feet away, the bartender found himself at a loss. He was choked with anger, with bitterness and a sense of betrayal, but he did not know how to begin, how to give these things utterance. Perhaps there was something insufficiently developed about his thoughts, or he'd simply not had time to process them. Perhaps, Jansen realized, his tongue was rendered paralytic by the same force that had halted his words since he was a child.

He went over and took a seat opposite Wisnat. The two sat staring at each other, at the walls, at the table between them. When Jansen could no longer take it, he leaned forward in his chair.

"Well?" he said.

"Well what?" replied his friend.

The bartender felt himself beginning a retreat, but then recognized he had to, regardless of the discomfort, make a stand.

"I saw what you did," he said.

"What *I* did?"

Jansen ignored this. "They were some kind of hair pill, weren't they? You gave her some kind of growth hormone."

Crossing his arms, the barber shook his head,

looked, in blatant disinterest, toward the window. "You, you, you," he muttered under his breath.

"All right then," said Jansen, "*we.*"

Wisnat gestured toward his friend. "Try and remember that."

"Why would I forget?"

"You're just as much to blame as I am."

"Maybe."

"No, not 'maybe.' "

"Fine," said Jansen, "I'm to blame."

Wisnat, momentarily appeased, wiped a hand across his face, and the two once again grew quiet. Jansen felt as if his efforts had been undermined, and looking at the barber something in him crumpled. He began to wonder if he could forget the events of the previous month, if they could just go ahead now that the unpleasantness was at an end.

"Anyway," he began in a friendlier tone, "I suppose it's over."

"Suppose what's over?"

"Megan," Jansen told him, motioning vaguely. "I suppose you're done with all of that."

"What makes you think I'm done?"

Jansen didn't understand. "I mean," he said, laughing nervously, "that that's usually it. Once you—"

"We didn't have sex, if that's what you're fumbling around."

The bartender simply looked at the man. He didn't understand this either.

53

"Then where have you been?"

"Excuse me, *Dad.*"

"I'm serious, Dennis. Where were you all this time?"

"I don't think I have to tell you."

"You were with her?"

The barber took a napkin from the dispenser and began tearing it into strips.

"You were with *Megan,* right?"

"You know, Jansen," Wisnat told him, "you're very fucked up."

"*I'm* fucked up?"

"Yes."

"What about you?"

"What about me?"

Jansen felt blood rushing to his head. He was angry, but there was something alongside the anger, something he'd not experienced even in the days when he witnessed his friend's conquests. He was, it briefly occurred to him, jealous.

"You want to keep seeing her?"

"It's none of your business."

"You're wrong," he said, "it *is* my business. You made it my—"

"Jesus."

"Please quit."

"Quit what?"

Jansen broke off, cast around as if looking for someone to assist. "Just give me an answer, Wisnat.

54

Just a plain, simple answer. Stop worrying about whether or not it's my—"

"Fine," said Wisnat, straightening in his chair and scooting to its edge, "what do you want to know?"

"Do-you-want-to-see-her-again?"

"Why wouldn't I?" he said.

"Because—"

"Because of the pills?"

The bartender nodded.

Wisnat looked to his feet. "That has nothing to do with it," he explained. "Is it that hard for you to understand me wanting to be with someone else?"

Jansen noticed that he was standing, though he would never recall rising to his feet. His breath was coming in spurts and his hands were shaking so badly that he grabbed the edge of the table to steady them.

"Why?" he managed, his voice starting to crack.

Wisnat sat for several minutes as if choosing, carefully, his words. Finally, he looked up at Jansen, gave a brief smile. He asked the bartender if it would be too difficult to believe that he might just be in love.

There followed a period Jansen could not remember, a stretch of compressed time, filled, he thought, with screaming and (perhaps) a momentary scuffle, twenty years of words spilling nonsensically and in no particular order from his mouth. When he came to, he had Wisnat by the collars, pressed against the wall. He was repeating the word *right,* unable to decide if it was a question or an answer or some ambiguous curse. Throughout, Wisnat's face remained surprisingly tranquil, as if this were something he'd been expecting all along.

Jansen grew suddenly quiet and his hands went slack. Wisnat took them carefully from his shirt and helped his housemate to a seat. The barber knelt in front of him, between Jansen's knees, placed a hand on either side of the man's face, cradling it almost. He exhaled a long breath, shook his head and then, with a resigned look — one that suggested having to finally speak of things better left unsaid — brought the bartender's face toward his, told him that he understood much more than Jansen thought. Wisnat explained that the darkness that hovered over him, had for the very first time lifted, that he could see clearly, as if the world had become transparent. He told Jansen that he had always been a good friend to him, that he appreciated it, but that all things drew toward an end. This, he explained, he must simply accept.

Finally, he told how there was something about Megan that Jansen did not yet comprehend, something he couldn't talk about, but that it made him feel necessary, almost *required.* Before Jansen could comment, before he could even open his mouth, Wisnat told him he need not worry himself over this. That he could be of no help in the matter. That such a thing could not be satisfied by one of his kind.

OCTOBER 5 OF THE subsequent year, Dennison Lee Wisnat and Megan Renee Thomas were pronounced man and wife. They flew out on a Thursday afternoon for Las Vegas, Nevada, and returned the following week. The gossip section of *The Perser Chronicle* mentioned that the two planned on taking as many trips as possible before raising a family. Jansen, reading the article several times before disposing of it, pondered the reporter's claim that this couple had a great deal in common. He could not, after some thought on the matter, help but agree.

He saw Wisnat very seldom over the next few years, but he would occasionally spy Megan on the street. The woman, it seemed, had undergone various changes: her skin much rougher than it used to be, almost leathern. Apparently, she spent her days in a tanning bed, wore makeup even more heavily than the last time Jansen had seen her at the bar. He would watch her go down the street, recede among the awnings and parking meters, unable to decide whether she looked happy or merely resigned.

Jansen could not pronounce judgment for he'd undergone a number of changes himself. That spring he put his bar up for sale and had little trouble getting rid of it. He felt, after all he'd been through, he needed time to recoup. But, although he altered his schedule and spent much of his time alone, he did not seem to be making progress toward recovery. He began taking long walks in which he would contemplate the events of the preceding year, trying to determine at what point he'd gone wrong, what potholed, gravel road he'd steered down to find the bridge out and the way back filled with insuperable barricades. At first he took his strolls in the country but soon switched to the sidewalks of Perser, starting just around evening when the streets were abandoned and the businesses closed, continuing, sometimes, late into the night.

There were aspects of the situation he could never understand. Why, for instance, when Megan had begun growing facial hair she did not choose to treat the problem medically. He realized what a blow such a thing must have been to a person with an ego as frail as Megan's, but were there not cosmetic remedies that would have made her right again? He'd seen ads for epilators and hair removal creams, an assortment of products she might have tried before succumbing to the barber. Perhaps, he thought, she'd tried some of these. Perhaps the chemicals that removed hair were less effective than those that claimed to grow it.

There were other things about the circumstances that Jansen failed to comprehend, but his walks were helpful in this regard. They led him, in due time, past the barbershop, and one night he made a discovery that seemed to bring things sharply into focus. He returned the next week at the same hour, saw that what he'd stumbled on was something akin to a ritual, and whether or not it was for the two who participated in it, it soon became so for Jansen: every Saturday and Wednesday for years to come.

Moving down the sidewalk just after ten, the streetlamps brightly lit, summer bugs or autumn leaves or winter flakes flitting about their bulbs, Jansen would come upon Main and follow it down to where Wisnat made his living, the same quaint shop with the plate-glass windows looking onto the street, the barber pole stationary now, the window shades drawn. There would be a warm yellow light coming from the edge of the blinds, and if one stood at just the right angle, one could make out what was happening inside without the slightest risk of being detected.

It was here that Jansen discovered what years of reflection had proven powerless to reveal. Here that he realized *gay* described his behavior better than most appellations. Here he understood that the love he bore Wisnat was inescapable, that suffering an existence of insult and desire was not the worst thing that could occur; that life, without love, without even the false hope of love, had very little left to it.

And now that he realizes this, is he better off for the knowledge? Has the epiphany fostered a clearer sense of self in this man who stands outside the barbershop with his face pressed against glass, watching past his blurred reflection, as he had from the backseats of teenage cars, Wisnat—the barber's expression strangely ecstatic these days as he looks to the woman reclining in the chair below him, covered in a long sheet, perhaps even naked beneath it. The former bartender watches with a yearning that seems to match the barber's rapture, watches as the man takes foam from the dispenser and removes the washcloth from Megan's face, her skin warm and red, steaming slightly in the summer air. The foam goes onto her cheeks, Wisnat working it carefully in, and then the razor, just as careful, moving gently across her face—smiling, Jansen supposes, though he cannot tell this either. It feels wonderful, Jansen can remember, moving a little closer, closing his eyes to better imagine the sensation, the sound. It was the sound he had not forgotten, that which remained etched on his memory, a sound like something being scraped away, a noise he'd associated, at one time, with being cleansed, washed, as a child at the altar, of his sins. And though he cannot hear it through the glass, can hear nothing but the wind or swell of cicadas, he knows the sound as he knows the voice of the man who produces it. The crystalline noise of those smooth, clean, strokes. That scraping of the razor, like fingernails on glass.

THE OFFERING

An image was before mine eyes, there was silence, and I heard a voice, saying, shall mortal man be more just than God? Shall a man be more pure than his maker? Behold, he put no trust in his servants, and his angels he charged with folly: how much less in them that dwell in houses of clay, whose foundation is dust, which are crushed before the moth? They are destroyed from morning to evening: they perish for ever without regarding it. Doth not their excellency which is in them go away? They die, even without wisdom.

— JOB 4:16–21

HER SURGEON HAD explained this procedure would take five hours—one to make the incision and remove the lamina, another to extract the disk, three more to position the bone grafts, fasten the vertebrae with pins and screws. When Kathy began to awaken, struggle against the blur of vision and sound, she saw white brilliance and a ring of figures brightly clothed, supposing, at the age of fifty-one, she'd expired on the operating table and ascended to her reward. Warmth overcame her and then elation, an assurance, as in those hymns she sang in church, that there was indeed a celestial paradise, and her voice, unparalleled in the congregations of Oklahoma, would attain its chosen place.

It was out of respect for this calling that she'd flatly refused her pastor's prompting to think toward secular venues. She sang, she informed him, as a type of ministry, and a performance of Wagner or Strauss would jeopardize the one gift she could offer. Her husband and daughter had argued against this, but now, as the bright forms encircling her grew clearer, she knew she had acted properly: her compensation would be great and the next face she saw, that of her Savior. Even as the notion suggested itself, a set of kindly features emerged from the radiance and drew close, a voice speaking in calm and measured tones, telling her not to worry, that everything would be okay.

"Mrs. Olaf," it said, "you shouldn't try and talk."

But Kathy tried regardless, the smile stretching the right half of her face beginning gradually to lower, the nurse providing details of her stroke.

WHAT, UPON AWAKENING, had seemed five hours was in truth a monthlong coma. During the laminectomy, Kathy's blood pressure had risen, and there was clotting just below her knee. The doctors had not understood what was happening until the anesthesia wore away and their patient lay unresponsive, her face vacant, eyes fixed to the wall. Through the years to follow, she would gather only the vaguest impressions of this time—a stretch in which dream bled to waking, color to speech, one afternoon a figure standing at the foot of the bed grasping her shin, asking could she feel this, and what about *now?*

But when Kathy did awaken, she did so fully, and the doctors were pleased to find that there was no damage to the brain, none to liver or kidney function, very little to the CNS. The left side of her body had been affected, but her recovery in this regard was just short of miraculous. A few days and she was drafting letters; within a week she was walking; after a month she was released from the hospital altogether. The stroke seemed now to involve only her larynx, her tongue and esophagus, most notably, her voice.

For the most, Kathy was able to suppress the terror such an affliction might have caused. The doctors said, given her progress in other areas, she could expect the complete return of vocal ability and in the meantime encouraged her to consult a speech therapist, which she did several times a week. Each morning she would awaken to find something else restored to her, another skill recovered. The left side of her face grew taut; she ceased to drag her foot; her penmanship continued to develop, then attained, almost, the precision of type. She kept pen and legal paper with her at all times, conversing, in this way, with her daughter and husband. Strangely, she found relationships with her family were strengthened, and viewing it as a temporary state of affairs, Kathy began to experiment. She left mischievous notes on her husband's pillow, scribbled reminders to her daughter, scolding her for a chore left undone, sneaking Post-its into her cereal box or bag of chips. On weekends, she would sit at her desk and write long letters to her mother and sisters, receive replies just as lengthy, speaking of matters they had not been able to discuss. In many ways, the silence that she viewed as a thing to be overcome had fostered a peculiar kind of intimacy. Driving home from the market one day, she realized that the anxiety attacks that had once forced her to carry Valium seemed to have vanished.

And yet there were nights she went to bed and an apprehension would vibrate in her chest, a flow of acid to her stomach, shortness of breath—the thought she might never again form words, let alone perform. She pushed this away, for the idea held a taint of blasphemy: she was chosen to bring song to the world, and this is what she would do; as long as she was alive, this is what she would offer. How could it even be otherwise?

Time passed. Eight months. Nine. Kathy awoke on a Monday morning with feeling in her tongue and throat. Her doctor removed the tube from her stomach through which she took food and put her on a liquid diet, then on solids. She was able for the first time to swallow and chew. At the table one evening, just before dessert, Kathy suddenly cleared her throat. There were a few moments of absolute silence, daughter and husband staring. They blinked several times, began slowly to clap.

Then came the one-year anniversary of her stroke, and in a weekly meeting with her therapist, the man informed Kathy that her speech might not return. She sat for a while, then nodded, went to her car and drove home. Walking inside, she stood a few minutes in the hallway, scanning the room—dining table and ottoman, recliner and venetian blinds, slats of sunlight dividing the carpet into a checkerwork of shadow. Her husband and daughter were not yet home, and there was, she noticed, a palpable silence, an absence that seemed to vacuum sound into it, to become, in some way, its negative. Blood rushed in her ears. Motes swirled in the afternoon light. When her husband pulled into the drive, Kathy was aware she had begun, after a fashion, to scream—hands clenched, nails cutting into her palms, no sound but the force of air across her teeth, the quiet hum of the refrigerator, the scarcely perceptible ticking of an antique clock.

SHE BEGAN TO FLOOD her environment with sound. There were the gospel tapes she played on her morning drive, the headphones in her office at work. She had a radio installed in the shower, a waterproof component that on most days was capable of nothing but static. Kathy listened to it regardless, steam beading the shower door, the water turned hot, aimed at her throat.

She became a compulsive watcher of television, she became a lover of malls. Even the Pentecostal church she had attended for the last twenty-seven years seemed far too quiet, the prayer service close to unbearable, and one night, unable to sleep, she saw a program wherein charismatics pranced in the aisles while a preacher stood singing above them, accompanied by an electric band. Kathy observed this with great attention. She fetched the remote from between two cushions, turned up the volume.

One afternoon, her husband—a squat man with thinning hair and glasses that slid incessantly down the bridge of his nose—arrived home late and, with a self-congratulatory smile, sat a cage in front of her, wrapped in silver paper, tied with a bow. Beside it was a smaller, rectangular package, likewise wrapped. Halfheartedly, Kathy reached from where she lay and undid the ribbon. Behind chrome bars, she saw a parrot—green and yellow—shifting from one leg to the other.

Kathy picked up her pen, scratched quickly at the tablet, held it toward Chris.

What the hell is that?

"Parrot," her husband told her. "You can teach it to talk."

Kathy stared at him a moment. She wrote the word *how.*

Chris smiled. Pointed. "Open the other," he said.

She did so and discovered, inside a padded cardboard box, a device roughly the size and shape of a book, though not nearly as thick. It was dark gray and had a speaker at one end. On its surface was a keypad, a small digital screen. Instinctively, Kathy moved a hand along its side, flipped a switch, and brought the screen to life, bright green letters asking her to enter a name.

"I got it at that store we went to over in Shawnee," Chris said. "The one with the wheelchairs?"

Kathy sat staring at the mechanism. She looked up at her husband.

"It's called a *talker*. They make them for people who lose their voice." Chris sank both hands in his pockets, began to rattle change. "I know you're going to get everything back, but for right now I thought it'd be nice not to have to write all the time."

Kathy forced her mouth into half a smile.

"Wouldn't it?"

She shrugged.

"Well," Chris said, sitting on the couch beside her, "they told me I could take it back if you don't want it. You might at least give it a shot."

Kathy looked back to the apparatus on her lap. She typed her name into the keypad, pressed firmly the button marked ENTER.

Ello, Kathy, the machine welcomed, metallic and harsh, a voice she'd almost come to expect.

SHE HAD HESITATED at first to even turn it on, to hear the device pronounce again those words and syllables that ought to have been coming from her. It found a place on the kitchen table beneath a stack of bills and flyers. One morning, she saw her daughter employing it as a coaster. There was a permanent ring on its display from her glass of orange juice.

It was the parrot that occasioned the machine's initial use. Kathy, after taking the week off, was lying on the couch watching television and, from the corner of her eye, the bird rocking nervously on its perch. When the program went to commercial, Kathy hit MUTE and turned her full attention to the parrot. She thought it peculiar the way the bird's eyes — glassy and dark — did not permit the expressiveness one associates with the eyes of a dog or cat. There was a vacancy to them, as if someone had taken a drill and bored holes in the creature's face.

Still watching the bird, she got up, walked quickly

over, and retrieved the machine out from under the catalogs and issues of *The Perser Chronicle*. She brought it to the couch, sat down, flipped the switch at its side. When the screen came up, she typed a phrase and pressed ENTER.

The bird stared at her blankly, shifting its feet. It cocked its head to one side and let out a brief croak.

Kathy retyped her message; did so again; was still doing this when Chris entered from the garage, stood next to the piano, and quietly observed the proceedings. He had just opened his mouth to ask what she was doing, when the bird, in guttural replication of the machine, uttered one of the words she'd been typing for close to an hour now. Kathy jerked her head toward her husband and smiled. She once again entered the phrase, and this time the bird repeated it in full.

Over the next week, Kathy would work with the parrot an hour each day. It was the first progress she'd enjoyed in quite some time, and though she pondered the reasons God would bestow such a gift on the bird and not on her, she hoped to make a good showing. Perhaps, she thought, it was a test. Maybe she would be rewarded for her selflessness, for considering God's grandeur and not her own. It was with this in mind that she sat down one afternoon when her husband and daughter were out shopping, pulled the machine onto her lap, and typed *Jesus is Lord*.

The parrot did not hesitate. In a voice that resembled, to an alarming degree, the machine's, the bird spoke loudly back to her the name Jesus.

It was harsher-sounding than she would have liked, but Kathy was pleased with her success. Nodding excitedly to her pupil, she retyped the message.

The bird looked at her, craning its neck. "Jesus," it shrieked.

Kathy continued typing and the bird continued repeating the name. She had been able to accomplish "pretty bird" and "who's that" and even "Chris and Kathy," but for some reason the parrot would not consent to follow "Jesus" with anything but the slight shuffling of its feet.

Kathy tried for a few more hours but could get nothing else from the bird, and by the time her husband and daughter arrived, she was weary to the point of tears. She stood, walked over to Chris, and put her arms around him.

"Hey," her husband asked, "are you all right?"

"Jesus," the bird interrupted.

Chris turned to look at the cage. The parrot rocked on its perch. "Jesus," it screeched.

"When you teach it to do that?" said Chris.

Kathy shook her head, made several indecipherable gestures.

Her husband laughed nervously. "Sounds like it's cussing. Like it dropped a hammer on its foot."

Their daughter, a pale-skinned teenager with a shapeless body and eyes that resembled in many ways the bird's, went to the cage, stuck a finger in between the bars, and attempted to stroke the creature's head. The bird inched to the far side of its perch, flapped several times its wings. "Jesus," it said, and with that sank its beak into the young woman's hand.

The parrot continued its blasphemous monologue through dinner and intermittently over the course of the evening, and that night even when they put the sheet over its cage and turned out the lights, its metallic voice would cry out, muffled a bit but piercing nonetheless. The bird had just seemed to calm itself, and Chris was on the edge of dozing when his wife broke down and began to cry hysterically. He eased over, took her head on his shoulder, and held her against his chest, beginning to whisper. But try as he might, his wife did not seem receptive to comfort, and eventually he began to grow upset himself. He scooted slowly back to his side of the bed and lay there, listening to her weep.

"Kathy," he said, after a while, "you need get a hold of yourself."

The suggestion only caused her to sob louder. Chris closed his eyes and tried to sleep. The bed began to tremble. Without the use of her voice, the noise sounded as if someone were attempting to strangle her.

"Really, now," he told his wife. "That's not going to help."

"Jesus," said the bird.

SHE DECIDED, IN the days following, she would have to make a stand. No more lying on the sofa cradling the remote, calling work at the last minute, telling them she'd not be able to make it. She had the impression she was beginning to sink, that if she closed her eyes, the recliner would make its way gradually through the floor. It was time, she thought, to stop feeling sorry for herself. It was time to engage with life. She felt like the curator of a forgotten museum, walking corridors and silent halls, occasionally dusting a sculpture, stooping to polish a fingerprint from glass, quiet caretaker scanning obsessively her collection, waiting for the day she would be replaced.

She started by returning to the gym, two hours a day, three on weekends. She did treadmill and weights, swam and tried step aerobics. Her back had begun to ache once more, but the exercise seemed to help this, and her mood improved greatly as a result of being on fewer pain pills. In the evenings, she and her husband would go to the park—something she'd rarely done since her daughter had been born. She had gone back to using the tablet, and it seemed more natural somehow, allowing her to articulate herself with precision. In support, her husband bought a notebook as well, and most of the time they would conduct their exchanges purely in writing. He claimed he felt guilty speaking.

Besides, he wrote, *I enjoy the quiet.*

And yet, despite the fact she'd recovered her morale, despite the improvement in her relationships, Kathy was increasingly plagued by the desire to perform. She could avoid the feeling for several days, and then she would hear a song on the way to work, see a singer on TV or at church, and there would be a sudden throbbing at the back of her skull, a sensation she would have to clench her teeth to avoid. It was not, Kathy would admit, that she was no longer able to minister. Neither was it about accomplishment. She came to understand that in singing, she received validation, a sense of being accepted. Only in that instant could she be, in any way, spiritual. It was her primary link to something larger, her only proof of the divine.

At the start of the next week, she met her pastor in his office. In times past, the man had been her biggest supporter, someone who had encouraged her to pursue singing as a career. After they'd exchanged pleasantries and she had scribbled answers to questions about her health, Kathy slid a note across the desk that expressed her desire to begin, once more, performing.

The pastor gave her a kind, confused look.

"Exactly what," he asked, "do you mean?"

She slid another note across, saying she had something in mind.

"What kind of *something?*"

Again, there came another note, telling him it was a surprise.

Kathy would never decide if it was mere pity on his part—or perhaps a vague desire to exploit the situation, to present this woman as someone who, despite her hardships, refused to be silenced, would express her thanksgiving even if she had to do so with sign language—but by the time she left his office, Reverend Hassler had agreed that a week from the following Sunday he would introduce her just before his sermon, provide whatever accompaniment she required. She told him she would need someone on the piano, that she would be in touch regarding which song.

Over the next two weeks, Kathy devoted several hours a day to practice. Her husband and daughter agreed during this time to remain in the living room, to make sure the television's volume was loud enough that they could hear nothing of her rehearsal. When, out of utter curiosity, Chris asked what it was she'd planned, Kathy smiled broadly and indicated that the secret nature of the enterprise would cause him to be all the more impressed when the day of her performance came.

He shook his head and told her he was impressed already. After all, it had been weeks since she'd broken into tears, and the parrot, having kept them awake several nights with its outbursts, seemed to have forgotten its new vocabulary altogether.

THE FIRST SUNDAY of July was hot and bright, Oklahoma summer, surprisingly humid. Kathy stood in the mirror, adjusting her dress, her sleeves and collar. Though her face had tightened a good deal since the stroke, she could still detect a slackness. She put a hand to her cheek, pulled the skin to achieve a tautness proper to her age, pulled more, hoping, in this way, to see back through the years. There was forty-two and, stretching further, there were her thirties—this was how she looked at nineteen. She let go her face and stepped backward. Taking up a large purse, she put an arm through its strap and turned to leave.

Her nerves were such that on the way to service she drummed her fingers in continuous motion on the armrest. At one point, she glanced over and caught her husband smiling. He reached, put a hand to her knee, and gave a gentle squeeze. In the backseat, their daughter asked if she could go to a friend's house for lunch.

By the time they arrived at the First Pentecostal, Kathy had fully installed herself in the mind-set of performance, a curiously numb state wherein she felt her muscles begin to contract, a means she'd devised of keeping anxiety at bay, failure from drifting into her thoughts. The family made their way through a barrage of handshakes and hellos, went to the sanctuary's far right, and seated themselves at the front. Smoothing her dress beneath her, Kathy caught sight of Reverend Hassler sitting on the platform. The man glanced over and cast an inquisitive look whose slightly raised eyebrows seemed to ask whether or not he was to go through with the plan as they'd discussed it, two days before. Kathy nodded.

She would never be able to recall the first part of that morning's service, though she knew the ceremony by rote—the ritual of hymns and offering, testimony and announcements. It had not been altered for as long as she'd been a member, and it suddenly occurred to her what she and the pastor had planned would constitute an extraordinary moment in the church's history. When he left his seat and approached the podium, Kathy's attention snapped to, the anxiety once again present. She raised a fist to her mouth and forced a cough.

"Brothers and sisters," the reverend began, "most all of you know Kathy Olaf, and you also know the incredible trial she and her family have weathered this last year. Sister Olaf has been with us for almost three decades now, and she's performed more solos than I can remember. When we heard of her stroke—when I heard of it, at least—I knew we'd lost something very special. I think, for many of us, it was one of those times that I spoke about last Sunday, one of those times when even those of us with great faith start to question things. I know I did."

The man paused, let his gaze sweep the congregation. Kathy watched intently, pleased with where this introduction was headed. She shifted in her seat, brought her purse onto her lap, and looked inside.

"But," the man resumed, "we have a real treat for you this morning. Sister Olaf approached me a few weeks ago, expressed how badly she wished to continue her ministry of song. And when I heard how she was planning to do it, I can't tell you how I felt. I guess, at that moment, I realized not only her dedication, but that her willingness to serve God and her refusal to accept defeat would continue to bring us blessing, perhaps even more than it did before her sickness. It gives me real pleasure to introduce Kathy Olaf to you and to announce a new era in her service of the Lord."

Kathy rose from her seat and was met with a roar of applause. It continued as she climbed onto the platform and stepped to the pulpit, as she brought the microphone to a position almost touching the lectern's surface. Even when she stood there motionless, smiling and raising a hand to the audience, the applause took a full minute to die down. She reached into her purse, removed the machine her husband had bought her, and slid it between the podium and microphone, and at this moment, understanding her intentions, the congregation began to applaud once more, some to whistle and cry out. When, finally, they had settled, she glanced to the pastor sitting behind the piano and motioned that she was ready. He began to play the intro, cautiously striking each note as if he were drawing the rhythm behind him on a string. Kathy nodded once or twice and then started rapidly to type.

She had chosen an older hymn, part of her repertoire from the days when she'd first begun to perform. She pecked out the opening verse, scarcely hearing the sound she made or even looking to see the crowd's reaction. *I come to the garden . . .* , she typed, *While the dew is still on the roses / And the voice I hear falling on my ear / The Son of God discloses*. Kathy had practiced many hours just to get to the point where she could make the machine keep tempo, and since she had no control over its pitch or tone, this was where she devoted her attention. As she worked her way through the lines, that feeling that was now a part of memory began steadily to return; for an instant she was transported, forgetting she had been the victim of a stroke. It was ecstatic—a sense of being controlled by something from outside, of herself being the machine on which another force was typing. She had never before felt so like an instrument.

When the song turned to the chorus, she took her eyes from the keypad, glanced briefly up. She was smiling, but the expression was quick to fade. All

78

around the sanctuary, people were wincing, sitting
with heads lowered, faces plastered with agonized
smiles. It was then that Kathy heard the noise she'd
been making—*He walks with me, and He talks with
me / And He tells me I am His own*—noticing, for
the first time, how the PA amplified the metallic
speech, changed its pitch, added a slightly guttural
distortion. She'd never found the tone pleasant but
had, after a while, grown used to it. Now she heard
it as a sound completely alien, as if her illness had
discovered its perfect articulation, an ideal voice.

Kathy began the second verse, trying to focus on
the performance, on the idea that her attempt alone
was important, that this is what would astound. Her
fingers began to feel like they were operating in-
dependently of her body, each digit under separate
command. She knew she was falling behind, losing
rhythm and her place in the song. *The sound of His
voice,* she hurriedly typed, *Is so sweet the birds hush
their singing.* She tried to start the next line, but at
this moment her hands seemed to lock, the muscles
to freeze. She stopped in midstroke, her fingers balanced over the keys, lifeless almost, as if afflicted with
palsy. Drawing them into fists, she blinked several
times and then looked toward Hassler, abruptly aware
that he too had stopped playing. When she glanced
back to the audience, she saw her husband and daughter were staring at the floor.

In a matter of seconds, the crowd would begin

sympathetically to clap, their applause rising louder as they attempted to drown the note of humiliation that somehow lingered, sustained by the burgundy carpet and curtains, the padded pews and offering plates. Kathy knew the ovation would come, that eventually the disaster would be pardoned, smoothed over, utterly forgotten. She knew that people would extol her courage, congratulate the performance as an obvious success, perhaps even, one day, ask her to repeat it. But now she looked out over the heads of these churchgoers, not only hearing but, in actuality, *feeling* the silence, noting it as a palpable, even substantial entity, a concrete and sentient force.

It was this, more than her illness or embarrassment, that she found terrifying. That sense of quiet that seemed to turn the congregation sitting before her into an enormous painting, she the lone visitor to some museum where humanity was framed, placed under glass, hung in perpetuity. Or maybe she was the canvas. Perhaps it was her on the other side of the velvet rope, watching as tourists walked continually past. KATHY OLAF, read the small brass plate, people nodding to partners and stroking their beards before moving to the next installation, leaving only the silence, wide and infinite — miles of it, centuries. It wasn't calm or tranquillity, the peace that an irksome voice encouraged her to be mindful of, let grow and develop, even welcome. For Kathy, it was merely silence — a quiet that would remain undisturbed until that day she heard the click of the Curator's heels, impeccable suit and tie, flashlight in his grip. He would arrive one afternoon with his assistants, pace the room and then pause, turning his beam squarely on the glass behind which she stood. Without further consideration, he would speak to the helpers, or even lift a hand and point, his voice quiet as a whisper, saying, *That one: take it down.*

AGAINST THE PRICKS

GABRIEL TOLD HOW for months he had lived in the anguish of sin and depravity. How he'd sold out his calling and the gifts of his calling and the price of his redemption. That he'd crucified the Son of God, put Him to an open shame. And though it was past, though he'd received forgiveness and had been washed by purest blood, he would confess it. He'd confess as it was ever with him.

It was two years ago—he was twelve then, the age of accountability—that the yearning first began, that he caved to it, sinning against his flesh. He'd be at his studies, after church, having memorized at that time up to Leviticus 5:3, and he would feel the craving like a sudden flame beneath his eyes. Clenching his jaw, he would grit his teeth, but there was no victory, and closing the Bible, he would rise from his chair, shutting the door, locking it behind him. He did not imagine a woman, nor did he think of Amy. He stood naked in the center of his room, his eyes fixed only to the ceiling's blankness.

Immediately, he began to pray against it. He would lie in the floor with praise music on the stereo, praying till he shook. *Lord,* he would pray, *take this evil out of me. I don't want it. I want to be clean and pure and walk forever in the Spirit. My soul is dirty and my heart is foul. Cover me with Your wings. Take my sin and make me like a child.*

He'd be clean for days, and no untoward thought would afflict him. Then, before he knew, it would be time for service, and afterward he'd be in his room with lotion in his hand and the door locked. The Spirit burned him to where he thought he couldn't take it, but he did not listen. Not until everything had come and gone. Not until he stood with his face drained and his eyes wet, feeling like he'd died again and risen.

SOME OF THIS, he said, had been his own nature and failing. It came from looking at catalogs and from hearing others on the school bus and from thinking on lust. It was sin carving him out, hollowing him so he'd be useless to God.

But a great deal had been because of Amy. Since nine years old she'd cast her widened eyes at him.

She was one year older—large in the bosom and hips. No makeup, homemade dresses draping against her ankles and wrists, she had waist-long hair braided in a thick, blond rope down the middle of her back. She'd watch him at the altars while he was praying and often would stop him in the foyer to talk about his faith.

There were times he would labor to understand why it was she bothered him, whether the way she looked or the way she looked at him or the expressions of others when she walked along the pews, unaware. Always with Amy the sense that she did not know, did not want to impress, could only be impressed upon, like thumbprints in candle wax. Whatever she was or felt, he knew it before she spoke, and there was a softness about her, as if seen constantly through a smeared pane of glass.

He tried to tell her how she tormented him. He'd tried at camp meeting and church camp and at dinner on the grounds. One afternoon—it was the summer he turned fourteen—while out in the parking lot waiting for their families, he decided he would explain how he needed to be left alone.

"Amy," he said, leaning against the trunk of his mother's car.

She turned to face him, and he began playing with the zipper on his Bible case.

"What do you think we are to each other?"

"We?"

84

"Me and you."

She smiled, squinted her nose. "What'd you mean?"

"Like—"

"Like a couple?"

He nodded.

"I don't know," she said. "What do you think?"

"About us?" he stalled.

"Mm-hmm."

"Being a couple?"

"Right."

He dropped his eyes to his feet and stood a few seconds, neither of them saying a word. When he looked at her again, she had leaned back her head, the sun lighting the transparent hair along her neck and cheeks.

He zipped his Bible shut, told her he had no idea.

IN HIS SPIRIT, he knew he shouldn't be entertaining such conversation. His mother said Amy was sweet and dedicated now but, like any woman, could one day turn loose and follow the path of sin. They'd talk about it when he was helping her fix dinner. His father had left a few years before. Since then, it was just he and Charlotte.

He could remember sitting on the kitchen step stool after church, chopping vegetables for stew: celery and carrot slices stacked alongside the cutting board like coins.

85

"Gabriel," his mother was telling him, "you need to watch that sort of girl. I've seen them ruin men. Completely *ruin* them."

He kept chopping.

"Your uncle Richard married a woman who seemed nice. After six months, none of us could be around her."

He quit chopping and looked up. "Aunt Connie?"

"No," she said. "This was his first marriage. This was Donna." Charlotte took the cutting board away from him and scraped celery into the pot. Frowning, she gave it back.

"I didn't know Uncle Richard was married before Connie."

"It wasn't good for him," she said. "When Richard got saved, we all decided not to talk about it. There's no need to bring up the past once it's under the blood."

"How long were they together?"

"Once it's under the blood it does not even exist."

"How long?" he asked.

"Three years," his mother told him, stirring the pot. "It nearly drove him to the madhouse."

He reached over, got several more carrots out of the bag, and started cutting.

"She'd come to the house in short shorts, whining around in that voice. Your uncle Keith and I tried to say something, but he wouldn't listen."

"How come?"

86

Charlotte stopped stirring and looked at him over the rims of her glasses. She taught English at a Christian high school, had cautioned her son about using incorrect grammar.

"Why not?" he said.

Gabriel's mother picked up the wooden spoon resting on a paper towel beside the stove. The spoon was wet and the towel clung to it. She snatched the towel away, smoothed it, and set it back on the counter.

"It was because of lust," she said. "I hate to say so, but it is only the truth. Your uncle Richard was afflicted by demons of lust." She walked over to the refrigerator, opened the door, stooped. "We couldn't have been more thankful when he divorced her and got his deliverance."

The boy thought he knew his uncle Richard; he used to pull Gabriel's wagon behind his lawn mower when Gabriel was small. He had a difficult time thinking his uncle had been afflicted by anything.

Turning on the stool, he looked at his mother. Her head was stuck inside the refrigerator, one arm braced against the door, fog rolling out from between her legs. He cut a slice of carrot, put it in his mouth and crunched.

"Gabriel," her voice echoed.

"Yes?"

"Don't spoil your supper."

• • •

It was early that summer, around the middle of June, that the Reverend Bobby Hassler announced their church would be starting revival. They hadn't had one in years, and he'd decided to bring in an evangelist, named Leslie Snodgrass, who was only fifteen. Hassler told them he would set the church aflame.

By that time, it'd become bad with Gabriel. He was sinning twice a day, and even when he'd ask forgiveness he knew it was useless. He told God it was too large for him, like the apostle's thorn. He copied out the passage in red ink, taped it to the mirror above his dresser: *My grace is sufficient for thee, my strength is made perfect in weakness.* Some nights when the moon was coming through his window, he'd lie in bed, scanning the words till he fell asleep.

The first night of revival, he was so tired he could hardly hold open his eyes. He'd been dreading the services, knew they only meant more time around Amy. When he walked into church that evening, he went and sat on the opposite side of the building but could not keep his eyes from creeping across the sanctuary, watching the smooth spot behind the girl's ear where her skin turned to hair. It took effort to shake his attention from it when the evangelist began to speak.

Leslie Snodgrass was short and pale, and his eyes were sunken into their sockets. He had the look of one who didn't spend time around others, and Gabriel caught himself questioning whether he'd undergone the same trials or whether he'd already overcome them. The evangelist's grandmother, with whom the boy lived, sat on the front pew with a tape recorder, pressing its red button whenever Snodgrass began to speak. She was a small, elderly woman, but she had a muscular look about her, and Gabriel's mother said she was a blessing because she reminded them of the way women used to be in the church — wise and sturdy, unshakable in the faith. For a reason Gabriel did not understand, Delores Snodgrass frightened him.

Snodgrass began that night by reading a verse in Hebrews, having everyone stand to acknowledge the Word. His voice did not sound small and shrill like they'd expected. It sounded much older, deep and firm, a little sad.

"For if," Snodgrass began to read, "we sin willfully after we have received knowledge of the truth, there no longer remains a sacrifice for sins, but a certain fearful expectation of judgment, and fiery indignation which will devour the adversaries. Anyone who has rejected Moses' law dies without mercy on the testimony of two or three witnesses. Of how much worse punishment, do you suppose, will he be thought worthy who has trampled the Son of God underfoot, counted the blood of the covenant by which he was sanctified a common thing, and insulted the Spirit of grace?"

With that, he bowed his head and started to lead them in prayer. Before Gabriel closed his eyes, he glanced across the room, noticing for the first time how small Amy looked. He could have picked her off the ground and held her.

Snodgrass finished praying, asked them to be seated, and started to preach. The first thing he said was that his sermon was not addressed to sinners in the audience. A revival, he told them, wasn't for sinners.

"Revival," he said, "is for those who have one time been awake and then, through carelessness and temptation and a lack of attention, have fallen back asleep. It isn't for those who've never been awake. Revival is for the backslider."

He went on like that, his voice becoming louder and more commanding as he went. After he'd been at it for fifteen minutes, preaching about falling away from the Spirit and the special punishments reserved for those who'd blasphemed, people began growing excited. Gabriel could see it moving among them like a wave, folks becoming agitated, shifting in their seats. And the longer Snodgrass spoke, the louder the elders shouted, the more Gabriel felt a pain growing deep in his stomach. His eyes started to ache, and by the end of the sermon he wanted to crawl between the pew cushions.

When Snodgrass gave the altar call, asking all of them to come in and rededicate their lives, Gabriel went up and knelt beside Thomas Campbell. He told God he was sorry for his sin and reprobation. He asked him to rebaptize him in the Spirit, to give him the strength to withstand the trial he was under. He prayed so fiercely that sweat beaded his forehead and neck; so long that when he looked up he and Hassler were the only ones left.

Directly, the pastor rose, went to the podium, and dismissed service. People stood, walked over, and began crowding around the evangelist, telling him how much they'd enjoyed his preaching, how strongly they could feel the anointing. Gabriel saw that his mother was waiting in line to talk with Snodgrass too, so he threaded his way down the aisle, went back to the foyer. He wanted to keep the burning of God's Spirit inside him.

He walked outside and sat at the bottom of the handicapped ramp. The night was warm and the noise of cicadas swelled in the field across the fence. He sat listening to them, hugging his knees to his chest.

In a few minutes they stopped, and he heard gravel crunch. Turning, he saw Amy coming toward him across the parking lot. She walked up, stood beside him.

"Isn't he good?" she said.

"Who?"

"The preacher."

"Yes," Gabriel said, "he is good."

She stood for a while on one foot. Then the other. "Do you mind if I sit?" she asked.

Gabriel looked at the ground, hoping she'd go away, but she did not. She squatted and sat next to him.

He didn't know what else to say, so they sat in silence. A few people came out, got in their cars, and left, but most were still inside. Gabriel was debating going back in, finding an empty room, when he felt Amy's hip brush up against his.

It was the first time a girl had sat so close, and it felt like electricity moving down his throat, into his stomach and hips. Part of him wanted to get away, save himself for the Lord and His Spirit, but the other part was on fire.

Gabriel was unsure how long he stayed like that, hip to hip with Amy on the ramp, never even glancing to his side. He sat thinking about how if they were man and wife, he'd undress her slowly at night, brush her hair like a china doll. He thought how they could lie in bed, reading aloud the Scriptures, that when they coupled it would be an act of worship.

The door opened. He turned and saw that Snodgrass had come out onto the porch. He looked over, noticed the two of them, turned and walked back inside.

"He's so good," Amy whispered. "I hope he stays longer than a week."

Later that night, Gabriel stood in the center of his room with dress pants shucked around his ankles, her voice going through his head like something hot and sharp.

THE NEXT WEEK, service for Gabriel was excruciating. Night after night, he'd sit listening to Snodgrass preach, watching folk crowd the altars to receive their blessing. The Spirit continued dealing with him, beckoning him to repentance, and he'd often kneel at his seat, asking God to spare his life and soul, the smell of his own sweat rising from the pew.

There was a darkness, he said, that covered you in the midst of sin. The deeper one goes, the cloudier it becomes, like walking through a world of ash. You begin to hate yourself, despising the weakness of the flesh, its wants and desires. Soon when the voices come to torment, you start wishing to be dead.

Gabriel was always unsure why he did not then repent, why he didn't make certain his salvation. Perhaps it was because he did not want to embarrass himself in front of the congregation. They'd known him as a somber young man, serious about his faith; to confess that he'd been living with sin would have made him look a fraud. Perhaps, and he said he was more ashamed to admit so, it was on account of his desire for Amy. He knew that the further he moved from God, the closer he would come to her.

Lying in bed after service was worse. It was there,

among the quiet of the house, that the Spirit would work hardest. His family had been known for visions, through his mother's line down. She had related many of these revelations, how his great-grandmother once fistfought the Devil when he came to her in the figure of a lion.

Being far from sanctified, Gabriel did not see the actual images that his forebears had. But in his mind the portrait of Hell was vivid, as if thrown against a screen. He saw endless dark beneath caverns of rock, torment of nail and tooth and flame.

One night, he became so frightened he walked down the hall to his mother's room and climbed into her bed. She allowed her son to get close, put her arm around him.

"Gabriel," she said, "are you okay?"

"I don't think so," he told her.

"What's wrong?"

"I don't know."

They lay there, listening to the crickets outside the window, a green light coming in, moonshine off the leaves.

"Do you know what?" she finally asked.

"What?"

"Sounds as if the Lord might be speaking to you."

He did not respond. Only he moved closer, burying his face in the pit of her arm.

• • •

I<small>T HAD BEEN</small> near the end of revival, and still, said Gabriel, God was pouring out His blessing: salvations and healings and baptisms in the Holy Ghost. Word of Snodgrass had spread, and quite a few had driven in from out of state. The sanctuary was full, and across the back Reverend Hassler had placed folding chairs, some along the walls. Gabriel had sat watching the people shout and sing, his jaw tight and his teeth clenched, choking down the Spirit.

He remembered the evangelist stepping to the pulpit that night, reading a passage from Acts, then having them stand to anoint the Word. His message was Saul on the way to Damascus, how, before an apostle, he'd been a persecutor of the Church. Snodgrass said that there were many sitting in congregations throughout the country who weren't any better, some a good deal worse.

"There are those," he told them, "who call themselves 'Christians.' They go through the motions. Many hold office in the Church: deacons, elders, ministers of music. To see them walk down the street you would not know the difference; they look spotless from outside—whitened sepulchers. But, as Jesus said of the Pharisees, inside are the bones of dead men."

Gabriel had listened to him, thinking about the gift Snodgrass had been given, how it must feel to be free from sin. When he looked over to where Amy sat beside her parents, he noticed she had her head tilted and her eyes trained, concentrating fully on the preacher's words.

"What's to happen to these half-Christians," Snodgrass was asking, "to these lukewarm children of God?"

Some in the congregation moaned. Elders shook their heads.

"According to my Bible, there cannot be a *lukewarm* Christian. According to my Bible, Jesus said he'd have us hot or cold, and were we lukewarm he'd spew us from His mouth."

Some shouted amens. Others began to clap.

For the next half hour he told the horrors of a believer separated from his God, how his tribulation is doubled because he'd at one time seen the truth. He told how each of his moments is spent fearing the justice of the Lord, mourning the loss of His divine company, but his pride will keep him from returning. Finally, he told of the place reserved for this man, alongside the Devil and his angels.

The longer Gabriel sat, the more he'd known his sin was not worth it; there was nothing worth spending an instant in Hell. Sitting there, he'd decided however great the temptation, he would leave his sin behind. He would resist the wiles of the Devil with the very violence of righteous indignation. Even if he had to cut his privates and fling them to the dogs, it would be better than the pain he had lived through. Or the pain to which he was going.

Still, he did not understand how it was that night that had compelled him and not another. It was not the guilt, for that was always present. It was not exactly fear or longing, nor was it the power of the evangelist's words. It was, it seemed, an assurance that grew inside, letting him know when he left his seat he would be forever released. He felt deliverance hovering, buzzing near the crown of his head, and by the time Snodgrass gave the altar call, so badly did he desire redemption, his hands were shaking, his legs and feet. He was ready to make repentance, and he did not care who looked on.

Snodgrass had them grow quiet, lower their heads in prayer, his voice going out over them like a warm breath.

"Every head is bowed," he told them. "Every eye is closed. Christians are praying. As I said the first night, I'm not talking to sinners. If there are those of you sitting here who've never known Christ, you're welcome to come and receive Him. But tonight, this call is for the backslider.

"Brother and Sister, you've lost your way. Satan has steered you from the path, stolen your heart from the Shepherd. Where you thought you'd find happiness and satisfaction was only heartache, despair. How long will you wander, with your own

heart in rebellion against you? How long will you resist the pull of the Holy Spirit, the gentle tugging at
your heartstrings? You don't need me to say Hell
awaits you; you're half in it already.

"I'll ask as Christ did Saul that day, knocked flat
of his back and blinded by the light of Heaven: 'Why
do you persecute me? Isn't it hard to kick against the
pricks?'"

That's when the evangelist asked if there were any
who had once known Christ, who would like to
make their way back to Him.

"I want you to raise your hand," he said. "Do not
be ashamed. Jesus said, 'Whosoever is ashamed of
me on Earth, of him shall I be ashamed before my
Father in Heaven.'"

He might have said more after that; he might have
said nothing. All Gabriel knew was when Snodgrass
asked that question, he'd stood from his seat, walked
the aisle, and knelt at the altar. Before his palms hit
wood, he felt deliverance seize him.

In a few minutes, there were hands all about him,
voices. They cried out to God for his salvation,
anointed his head with oil, rebuked the powers of
Satan. One man whom he'd never seen put out his
arm, hugging Gabriel almost beneath him, telling all
the devils of Hell that he was God's by the power of
the Almighty Spirit.

They prayed for a long time. He wept until no
weeping was in him, and when he stood, a fire was

burning in his heart as never before. He walked back to his seat feeling light, as if he might crumble into air.

As church was dismissed, Hassler reminded them that the women had brought dishes. They were to meet in the fellowship hall, those who could. Many of the elders came and hugged Gabriel, said he would be in their thoughts.

He went back to the hall, sat with his mother while she talked to friends. There was only tea to drink and he was very thirsty, so after a while he went out to the foyer to get a sip from the fountain. Amy was standing there, the very look of holiness on her face.

They went out the front door, down the steps, around the side of the building. Someone had ran an extension cord into the trees, hung a bug zapper from the limb of a black oak. The lamp sparked and crackled as they walked, blue light tracing Amy's outline against the darkness.

When they reached the propane tank sitting at the edge of the property, Amy turned to face him.

"Gabriel," she said.

"Yes."

"What's it like for you?"

An insect hit the lamp, snapped against it. He felt stars blazing high above him.

"What's what like?"

"The Spirit?"

Gabriel thought about her question. "I don't know," he told her. "It burns."

"For me it's like something making me calm."

He didn't know what she meant.

"It's like there's a warm feeling, making it so I'm relaxed." She placed her hands on her stomach, smiled. "I feel it right here."

Gabriel saw how her face shone blue in the light of the bug lamp, her hair and eyebrows like blue suede. He wanted very badly to leave, the voice inside telling him so, but he pushed it down, moved closer, and then the voice grew quiet, went dead altogether. The two of them stood breathing the other's breath, and then Amy brushed his cheek with her nose. Her lips came near and his mouth went to hers, tiny fingernails scraping his hands. Straightaway, he felt the glory go out of him, replaced by the death of the world. He wanted to weep, seeing the glory go.

Amy shifted her weight, began to put her arms around his neck. But that, he would tell them, was when his deliverance had risen up. He shut his eyes, pushed her away, and kicked her in the stomach. He did not think about it. He just closed his eyes and kicked.

When he opened them, the girl was on the ground with her legs stretched in front of her, as if ready to play jacks. Her dress was hiked around her knees, her braid flipped over her shoulder, hanging into her lap.

Gabriel watched her for several minutes. Then he walked and stood over her, looking down in the grass.

"You kicked me," she said.

"Are you all right?"

"Why did you kick me?"

He squatted, sat on his heels. "Are you okay?"

She mumbled something.

"What's that?"

"I think so."

He sat there, pulling up grass and twirling the blades between his fingers.

"You can't say anything," he told her—saying nothing himself through all the years to come.

"About what?"

"This."

She shook her head.

"It won't help you, Amy. Even though it doesn't make sense, one day it will. This will be one of the best—"

She began to cry. One minute the girl looked as if trying to solve a math problem; the next she was crying. Gabriel reached and put his hand on her shoulder. She moved away.

"Promise me you won't tell, Amy."

She sat, wiping at her face.

"Amy," he said, "*promise.*"

She pressed her palms into her eyes, began rocking back and forth.

"Listen," Gabriel told her, "you're okay. Just promise me you'll not say anything."

She drew her hands from her face and looked at him for a very long time. He thought that she would then make her promise, but it cost him more coaxing to receive it.

I LEFT HER, he told the deacons, lying there, and walked back to the church. The trees were thick, and the light from the front of the building made a path along the grass, glowing out across it like God's sweet breath.

When I came round the corner, Brother Hassler was on the porch with Leslie. I walked up past them and went through the double doors.

Soon I passed the fellowship hall where people laughed and ate. From farther down, I could hear Mama, laughing and eating too.

In the sanctuary, all the lights were dimmed. I went up the center aisle with my dress boots making prints in the carpet. At the front, I squatted and sat cross-legged between the pews and altars. The wood was shining on the pulpit and all along the walls. It was polished, and in its grain there were faces. I sat making faces out of the grain, then turned so I could focus.

I closed my eyes. The smell of the sanctuary was

strong and the sound of it was quiet. Outside, the night was warm and quiet, like being put under water. I sat there, cross-legged and quiet—not to be touched.

She, I thought, could have it. The world and sin and death. And me, if I was let, I'd stay here and live off of what I felt burning inside. I'd take my burning, if God asked, and spread it; I'd let my fire burn evil out of everyone. And God, I knew, would strike them if they tried to take the fire away.

TRUCK

DAY OF UNCLE Kenneth's funeral. Ceremony in a country church. All around an abundance of wreaths and relatives, people I've felt guilty for avoiding. In their thrift store suits they look like straw men, like figures out of dreams. Charles is here with his autistic son; Thomas with his oxygen mask and Bible. For several minutes I watch Ronnie come down the aisle on his walker, wondering how long he's moved this way, how long he's been reduced to spectacle. Did it happen gradually, I wonder, his steps growing smaller and smaller until he appears, on this morning, to be walking in place? Jesus, my mother continually reminds me, was sent to heal such folk—the lame and the halt, the browbeaten and troubled of spirit. She bases her life on this conviction, believing her family's misfortune evidence of trial or punishment. To me, it only seems the Bartletts have been overlooked.

It isn't that I think I'm above them. Despite my graduate degree, my editorship at the local newspaper, I feel far from superior. I simply hate to see humans so superstitious, so thoroughly defeated. Ask any of them and they'll tell you, from the first day until now, Satan has administered a beating: not their wretched health-care system or lack of interest in higher ed, not the conservatives they're conned into voting for, the evangelists who cash their checks. It's the Devil they blame—red suit and horns, pitchfork and flames. Over the years, that imaginary threat has become crucial to their sense of doctrine. *Beware of the closet,* it tells them. *Fear sunset and the darkness beneath your bed.*

My mother's uncle, my great-uncle Kenneth, was the only one to go against this thinking. He was thrice married and divorced, continued smoking unfiltered cigarettes even after his surgeon confiscated a lung. Naturally, our family despised him for it. Even Mother, who underneath her religiosity is a kind and intelligent woman, even she declined to visit him the fifteen years after he moved back to Perser and lived alone on his ranch. Looking at my watch, seeing service will start in a few minutes, I realize that maybe she's decided not to come. Maybe she's refused to pay this heathen her respects.

She wasn't always this way. My entire childhood she thought church unnecessary, her Christianity composed of the typical clichés about doing unto others. But after Father died—the same autumn Kenneth moved down and bought his ranch—she began to go three times a week: Sunday morning and night, Wednesday evenings for potluck and singing. I thought it was her way of expressing grief. I was sixteen at the time and consoled myself with school-work and grades, applications to college. By my senior year I'd received a scholarship from the Jour-nalism Department at the University of Oklahoma. I walked in to tell Mother and found her sitting at the table, praying over handkerchiefs and putting them in the mail.

In a way, I felt I lost her then, both parents in the same year. Never mind that she was still breathing, raising a garden, and going to lunch with friends. Whenever I stared in her eyes, got close enough to see my own reflected back, I knew something had left. Much of the time, she reminded me of the fa-miliar house on the block that a new family moves into and makes unrecognizable. It's the same struc-ture, same paint and lawn. But the presence of the occupants changes the building so completely that it suddenly feels from another country. It even has a different smell.

Hearing a sound like something dragging carpet, I turn to see ushers closing the sanctuary doors. They walk down opposite aisles and take seats at the front of the church, begin to watch, along with the rest of us, a portly gentleman rise and make his way onto the platform. He has thick glasses, a thick head of hair slicked toward his crown. I can tell he feels awkward performing the service. Grasping the edges of the podium, he forces up the corners of his mouth, eyes trailing to the casket below him.

As he leads us in prayer, I think how I've seen such glances before—reverent and troubled, anxious beneath the facade—men who suppose they're looking at the shells of sinners, spirits writhing in an eternal blaze.

I SPEND THE REST of the afternoon trying to reach my mother, slipping away from the reception hall to a chipped pay phone in the breezeway of the community center. The phone just rings, and when I try an hour later, I get a busy signal. At home, it's the same buzzing, so that evening I drive over to check on her. I have to knock several times before she answers and lets me in.

Standing in the hallway, still in my dress clothes, I allow Mother to walk on ahead as I take a few moments to examine pictures on the walls. When I was a child, she began framing photos of our relatives. Now there are hundreds nailed up—you can track any family member from old age to youth. The ones nearest the door are black and white, photographs of people dead by their fifties. But as you walk, the pictures become color. There are ones of mother as a very young woman, a slim girl in a flowered dress standing on the running board of a Plymouth. Next to these are photos of her brothers, a sister I was never able to meet. Janet committed suicide in her twenties, hanging herself from the cedar in front of her house. She looks a good deal like Mother, though her features are a bit darker and she's fuller through the hips. There's a nice photograph of her as a child, sitting on a pier in shorts and bathing suit, feet dangling in black water. It's one I've studied a thousand times, though I continually forget to ask Mother where it was taken. In it, Janet's laughing and glancing to her side, eyes crinkling at their corners. Someone has placed an arm on her shoulder, but here the photo cuts off. I stare at the arm and then a few more pictures, trying to find one of Kenneth. Finally, I pull myself away and walk down the hall toward the living room.

Being inside the house has become stranger of late. It sometimes strikes me that everything about my life has advanced, changed in various ways, but Mother's home is roughly identical to how it's always looked. The carpet is the same orange-and-brown shag, the shelves stacked with the same knickknacks. The television is a Sony — I bought it for her last Christmas — but you can still see the twenty-year indentations from the old set. When I walk by the kitchen, I notice a box of cereal on the counter, this counter the same metallic flake I remember slicing bread on as a child. It takes me a while to register that the cereal—advertisements for cell phones on the front—is actually from this decade.

I walk into the living room and settle into Mother's recliner, begin listening as she tells me about her day. She's sitting on the couch beside me holding a glass of water, one leg crossed beneath her, left hand at her brow. Her fingers are cupped slightly around her eyes, as if shielding them from a glare. Although she's gained weight in recent years, she's still quite pretty—elegant eyebrows and skin, an oval face embedded with bright pupils. She's nearly seventy and for thirty years has dyed her hair jet black. I study the crushed-velvet look of it and, after she's meandered through various topics, turn the conversation toward the funeral, asking rather bluntly where she was. Not seeming to have understood my question, she gives me a puzzled look.

"Today," I explain. "Kenneth's funeral."

She nods, and for a moment I'm not sure she's going to respond. I'm about to begin a different approach when she tells me she's not been feeling well.

"What's wrong? Is it your stomach?"

"No, no, Spencer. Just tired. Think I'm trying to get a cold."

She explains there's a flu going around her church, a subject that leads to a series of fairly involved stories about people I've never met.

The entire time she's talking—and it's often this way with us—I attempt subtle gestures to indicate I'd like to turn the discussion back to a previous topic: clear my throat, begin nodding, scoot to the edge of my chair. But this does nothing, and soon I'm forced to interrupt.

"I really wish you'd been able to make it," I tell her. "The service was nice."

She nods.

"They had more flowers than I've seen at a funeral, wreaths and stands of gardenias."

She says it does sound nice, asks if I'd like something to drink.

"No. Really, I'm—"

"I just made a fresh pot of coffee and I have orange juice and prune. There are some beautiful apples I got on sale yesterday. Here," she says, standing, "I want you to look at these."

I follow her into the kitchen, trying to figure a way of expressing my disappointment without causing an argument, watch her slice an apple neither of us will eat.

She sets it on the table and we both pull back chairs, staring at the fruit, listening to the refrigerator hum. She begins to relate a conversation she had with a black man at the store, how she told him she didn't understand why they wanted to be called "African Americans." I nod from time to time to indicate interest.

After fifteen minutes have passed, I push back my chair and tell her I need to go, ask if she'd like me to take her to breakfast in the morning. She says she's sorry, that she can't, has to be up early to help with a yard sale at church.

"You know," I warn her, "if you're coming down with something, maybe you ought to take it easy for a few days. You don't want to go and make it worse."

She looks up, creases her brow, and I can tell, for a moment, she doesn't know what I'm talking about. Then her forehead relaxes, and she reaches out to squeeze my arm.

"I think I'll be just fine," she says.

TWO WEEKS LATER—fast food and alimony, editorials that elicit calls from members of the city council—I'm standing in my driveway inspecting a metallic green truck. I've just learned that before he died, Uncle Kenneth visited his lawyer and had the vehicle assigned to me in his will. The truck is a 1970 Ford, an extended cab with dual exhaust and polished chrome mud flaps. It has a toolbox that runs the width of the bed, side mirrors the size of cutting boards. Paint is just beginning to flake around the gas cap, but for the most part the pickup is in excellent condition. Kenneth's attorney called me about it yesterday afternoon, and today—still dazed, full of skepticism and interest—I woke early and had a friend drive me out to get it. Sitting next to my Volkswagen, framed by lawn and pavement, it looks horribly out of place.

I walk back inside, take a beer from the fridge, and study the truck from out my kitchen window. This morning, I was shocked to think of myself in possession of the vehicle, but standing there it has begun, almost, to grow on me. I can't imagine precisely why Kenneth willed me the pickup, but my guess is that he branded me a fellow in the cause and wanted to make a contribution. There had been several reunions where he complimented me on columns I'd written—columns on gun control or minority rights, the antiunion stance of most Oklahomans. Slowly, I begin to feel the gift is a bestowal of karmic goodwill, a sign from beyond the grave that I'm serving the gods of ethics and taste. Holding the beer toward the ceiling, I perform a silent and impromptu toast.

That evening I drive the pickup over to Mother's, park in view of the front windows. I often surprise her after dinner, offer to take her for ice cream or a walk, but today my motives are skewed. I want her to see the truck, to indicate some amount of guilt for having missed the funeral. I want her to admit how terribly judgmental she is, how self-righteous and smug. At the very least, I want her to see that despite his lack of religion, Kenneth was a generous man.

I go up the sidewalk and tap the doorframe. I can hear the noise of television from the living room, the cadences of a preacher, so I walk around back. She spots me through the glass door and slides it open.

"Spencer," she asks, "were you just around front?"

"Yeah," I say, stepping into the air-conditioning, "I knocked."

I see she already has on a housecoat and slippers, but her hair and makeup are done. "Sorry about that," she says, laughing. "I just took out my hearing aid." She goes over to the coffee table, turns down the television, and places a small plastic nub inside her ear. "It makes me nervous when I'm here by myself."

I fall into the recliner, flip the handle at its side. "You feel like ice cream?"

"Do I feel what?"

"Like ice cream."

She turns the knob on the hearing aid until it squeaks. "I'd need to put on some clothes."

"We can just go to the drive-through if you want."

"No. It's half melted by the time they hand it to you out that window."

She gets up, goes into her bedroom to get dressed.

I press the mute button on the remote, noticing how different the preacher looks when you can no longer hear him. Then, suddenly remembering, I turn off the set, walk down the hall, and go back and forth among the pictures till I find the one of Janet.

"Mom," I call. "Where was this photograph taken?"

"Where's who?"

"This picture of Aunt Janet?"

"I can't hear a word you're saying."

I lift the frame from the wall and take it down to Mother's room. She's on the side of her bed in tan slacks and a blouse, buckling shoe straps around her ankles. When she looks up, I show her the picture.

"Where was this taken?" I ask.

"Cleveland," she tells me, concentrating on her feet.

"Uncle Kenneth's old place?"

She nods.

"I didn't know he had a lake."

"Well," she grunts, "he did."

"Was it big?"

"I never went."

"He never invited you?"

She shakes her head, stands and smoothes the front of her slacks.

"Why did he invite Aunt Janet and not—"

"Spencer," she interrupts, "I don't remember. That was fifty years ago. Jan was nine or ten when that was taken."

We walk back into the living room and I watch her sort through her purse, remove the items she wants, and place them inside another. We start up the hall and I rehang the picture, open the front door. Mother steps onto the porch and pauses.

"Where's your car?" she asks.

"There," I say, pointing toward the truck.

Mother squints, furrows her brow.

"It's Kenneth's," I tell her. "He gave it to me in his will."

Slowly, she cranes her neck, glaring up at me, and for a moment my stomach sinks. It's like facing an adult after you've smashed a car window. Then this feeling fades, and I begin to grow angry. I want her to drop the pettiness, the righteous indignation. I want to tell her she should act more like the person her religion is founded on. But instead, I just ask if she needs help getting in.

She shakes her head.

"Mother—"

"You go without me."

"Please don't be like that."

"Spencer," she says, squeezing past, "I'm not going to hear any more about it."

She goes inside, leaves the door cracked a few inches. Soon, I hear the television come back on, the preacher's Southern lilt. I reach inside, turn the lock, close the door to, and walk back down the steps.

By the time I pull away from the curb, I'm so

angry my hands are shaking. I stop at the intersection, consider going back and having her explain to me why she's too good to ride in a dead man's truck. I sit with the engine idling, watching as a pack of children runs down the lawn next to me. They move in single file, their arms extended like wings, the one at the rear trailing a toy on a length of string. They circle and then come about, crossing the street, going up the opposite lawn, disappearing behind a hedge. I look after them for a while and then reach up, draw down the gearshift and put it into drive.

TODAY IS SUNDAY, hot and bright. I make coffee and lounge in my sweats, read till a quarter past noon.

At one, I walk outside and circle the pickup. I open the passenger door and slide across the seat, noticing the layer of dust on the dashboard, the interior dull-looking and grim. I swipe a finger across it, rub the powder into my thumb. Opening the ashtray, I find a number of butts, the glove box brimming with receipts and playing cards, a tire gauge. I go back in the house and rifle through the utility closet. Ten minutes later I'm outside again, garden hose and bucket, Armor All and chamois. I wash the truck from license plate to hood, use my shop vac on the carpet.

There's a layer of sludge in the bed, and it's pitted with bottle caps and acorns, crushed cans, faded bits

of mail, twigs, empty tins of Skoal. I lower the tail-
gate and spray everything into my drive, sweep it
into a pile, scoop it in the Dumpster. I examine the
dints in the bed, the rusted spots, wondering how
much it would cost to have them repainted. Prying
the locks on the toolbox lids—there's no key for
them on the ring—I find that Kenneth has left me
various tools about whose uses I can only speculate.

Behind the seat there's an ice scraper and jack, a
pair of jumper cables, a wrench with a red rubber
handle. There are also a number of smaller items—
tape measure, chalk, mismatched gloves—and I pull
a shoebox from underneath my bed, pile them inside
it. I lock the doors, carry the box inside, and toss it
on the living-room table. It's five till four and I'm too
exhausted to think about fixing dinner, about going
to see Mother afterward. Though our argument was
several days ago, I'm still having imaginary conver-
sations with her, dreaming of insults I'll never use.
Not wanting to consider it further, I take the pack of
cards from the top of the shoebox, open it, and slap
the contents into my palm. I begin to shuffle, then
flip through and study them one by one.

As a child I'd collected cards. Not having a brother
or sister, I spent a great deal of time developing
tricks, playing solitaire. When we would take trips
across country—Six Flags, Silver Dollar City, Walt
Disney World—I would make Mother buy a different pack in each state. I have stacks of them in a

closet somewhere, from casinos in Atlantic City and Vegas. It was, I'll admit, a rather useless hobby, but the tricks I learned made it seem worthwhile, and every month I'd invent a new one, take the cards to school and show friends. I relished the looks on their faces when an ace from a crisp Taj Mahal deck turned up where it shouldn't, when four kings from a Bally's pack—bright white and red—lined up beneath their noses. But these cards, Uncle Kenneth's cards, are like none I've ever seen.

This has nothing to do with the fact that on the back of each there are photographs of naked women: I have similar sets that friends ordered me from *Playboy*. Nor are the depictions particularly lurid. Kenneth's women adopt the standard poses, sit on their shins with their backs to the camera, stand with their hips projected and their legs slightly crossed.

What is troubling about this deck of cards is that in each of the photographs the eyes of these women have been blacked out—a thin, dark line obscuring their glances, a perfectly rectangular blindfold drawn across their vision. I can't quite understand why the image upsets me, and I go through the pack slowly, looking at each photo, trying to decide.

I am so absorbed in this, so thoroughly unsettled, that when the air conditioner kicks on, I feel as if someone has attached an electrical cable to my back, sent a charge to the base of my spine.

I'M IN MY OFFICE the following Tuesday when my cousin T. J. calls. He informs me that the family is auctioning Kenneth's estate, that a number of our relatives are meeting at the ranch to prepare his things.

"You know Uncle Ken," he says, as the conversation's about to conclude. "Wasn't much on housekeeping." He clears his throat and gives a nervous laugh. "I bet it'll take us most the weekend." T. J. drives a semi, works as assistant pastor for a Fundamentalist church in the town adjacent. There are insinuations in his remark that I far from appreciate, the Puritan implication that physical untidiness has its spiritual counterpart. But I let it pass, tell him I'll be out at seven thirty to help. He thanks me and asks how Mother is doing. I skirt the question, let him know about receiving the truck.

I write my column in fits, typing a few words as they come. I keep thinking of the playing cards, the apparent fact that my uncle relieved the loneliness of his existence with pornography. This is something I have little problem with, but as the hours pass, an anxiety begins to grow in the back of my thoughts: if Kenneth, I hypothesize, kept such items in his glove box, there's no telling what we'll find in his closets. My family will finally be able to level specific charges, and his liberalism will be seen as indicative of even more sinister transgressions. I can't, I decide, allow this to happen, feeling that a strange bond has grown between us, that it's my responsibility to defend him, conceal anything that might cause embarrassment. Of course, I realize it doesn't matter in the least, that he's finally beyond their reaches. Still, his is a memory I'm compelled to protect.

So my plan is to drive out to Kenneth's Friday evening before any of my relatives get there and sift his belongings, dispose of anything they might deem incriminating. Surely, even the most enthusiastic collector can't have accumulated more pornography than I can manage in a few hours of intensive cleanup.

That evening I drive over to visit Mother, this time in my Volkswagen. I find her tending the garden. She seems glad to see me, as if she too wants to dismiss our spat. We make lemonade, and then I sit on the porch and talk with her as she waters. We discuss events from her childhood, her brother's windfall in the stock market, something humorous her father once told her, and for a few moments we're actually having a relaxed and enjoyable time. I even become excited, thinking our relationship has broken some insuperable blockade. Slapping a mosquito into my thigh, I begin to laugh.

But after a while, this starts having an opposite effect, and despite myself, I start growing angry, feeling more strongly than ever that Mother's religion has kept us apart. There's only so far any conversation can take us, and even though she's chuckling now, I know some offhand phrase could be used as invitation for attack, a plea that I start attending church or to my soul.

Picking up my glass, I walk back into the house and stand for a while at the kitchen sink. I look down the hall where the pictures begin, thinking that things might have been different if Father hadn't died. For the first time in years, I find myself missing him, the sound of his voice. I can remember all of us together, how Mother seemed then, nuzzling herself beneath his arm on the way home from movies, sitting in a folding chair, overseeing his work on a car.

Looking up, I see her dragging the hose across the lawn. I watch as she pulls it to a flowerbed, twists the nozzle and, when nothing comes, realizes there's a kink cutting off the pressure. She raises the hose and snaps it, trying to whip out the knot, reminding me of I don't know what with the sleeves of her housecoat flailing and a pained expression on her face. Finally, she lays the nozzle in the grass and dis-appears beyond view of the sliding glass doors. I continue watching it, that small piece of brass a few yards from the concrete, buried, almost, in green. Suddenly, it moves several inches on the end of its hose—then a foot. Water begins to fan from its spout, spraying partly into the ground, partly in an arc against the side of the house. I'm about to walk over and turn it off when Mother moves back into the frame, stooping to retrieve the hose, smiling.

• • •

THE SUN IS GOING under by the time I get off work. Kenneth's ranch is six miles to the north of town, a half mile east. There's a blacktop off 99 that turns to red dirt and gravel, ditches with sumac shrubs, berries coated in dust. The oaks out here are thick and with the windows down I can hear katydids above the sound of my engine. Dusk is settling among the trees and bushes, blurring out the edges of the leaves. At the bottom of a small valley is the driveway to my uncle's house. I pull in to find the gate closed, padlocked. Stepping out of the car, I climb the fence and start up the clamshell drive, the moon just now coming over the tree line.

Walking around a bend in the road, I see Kenneth's house, back in a clearing among the trees. The yard is unkempt, dandelions and milkweed, but I can tell from an outside lamp that the power's still on. I'm reassured by this, glad I don't have to move about the house with the flashlight I've brought. I've never been overly fearful of such things, but there is something about the house I find unearthly, edged as it is by tangled limbs, the noise of crickets. Reminding myself I've seen too many horror films, I step onto the porch and move up to the door. Before I can catch myself, I've already knocked.

There are several keys on the ring and one of them slides easily into the deadbolt. I push the door and it moves soundlessly on its hinges. Inside, I quickly find a lamp, then a switch that throws on another. In the yellow light fanning from their shades, I see that I'm standing in the living room of a common farm-house: rustic paintings and rocking chairs, a set of mahogany bookcases filled with classic novels and plays. I walk over and run a finger along their spines, hoping to be able to persuade my relatives that they should go to me. On the third shelf is a book I re-member enjoying as a child, a mystery of sorts by V. Thomas Maas. It too is filled with old houses and secrets, creaky staircases, the intimation of ghosts. Flipping the pages, I find a passage I vaguely remem-ber, a scene where the protagonist searches his grand-mother's library for the book he believes will contain an important letter. I read it slowly, a smile widening my face as the character pulls volume after volume from the shelf, unable to discover the object of his quest. Wishing there was someone to share this, I put the book back in its place, turning behind me to glance around the room.

As badly as I hate to admit it, T. J. was right about the housekeeping. The house is remarkably untidy, a layer of dust over everything, a smell of inactivity which I try not to associate with death. There are cardboard boxes half filled with magazines—*National Geographic* and *Harper's, The Nation* and *Time*—cases of what look to be batteries and art supplies, sacks of kitty litter, cat food, and treats. I begin to wonder who took care of Kenneth's cats, and I'm suddenly worried I might run across a carcass, afraid they may have been locked inside. I look over and see a small door with a plastic flap cut into one wall, decide that they've long since deserted.

I sit down in one of the rockers, attempt to develop some type of a plan. Finally, I can't see any other way except to examine every cranny and hiding place. I start with the hallway closets, fairly empty except for a few shotguns, an expensive-looking rod and reel. I move on to the bedrooms, the dresser drawers, between the mattresses, under the beds. In what I take to have been Kenneth's room, there's a small nightstand in which I discover pairs of tube socks and an envelope filled with black-and-white snapshots. Flipping quickly through them, I see they're only family photos, many duplicates of the pictures Mother has on her walls. I pocket these, deciding she might, at some point, want to see them.

I go in the kitchen, search the cabinets and beneath the table, even climb a ladder into the attic, seeing nothing but pink insulation, two-by-four trestles, and pinewood joists. Out back of the house, in Kenneth's work shed, I find welding equipment and odd-looking tools, an ancient saddle with intricate stitching. Coming inside, wiping sweat from my neck, I make a last sweep through the house: couch cushions and medicine cabinet, under the furniture and sinks. I look at my watch and see that I've been at it for an hour and a half, having turned up nothing remotely indecent. Sitting once again in Kenneth's rocker, I begin to feel rather guilty. There's no way to know precisely where the playing cards came from, how they found their way into the glove box, whether or not my uncle even knew of their existence. Turning off the lights and locking the deadbolt behind me, I walk back down the drive, coming to the gate in the full glare of the moon.

On the way home and then later at the house, I consider my hypocrisy, how I too had judged Kenneth. I wonder how much there is about *me* that's in need of exorcism, to what extent I've been contaminated by my family's ethics. I pour myself a drink and ease into the recliner, begin to think, once again, about finding my way out of this town, applying, perhaps, for an editor's position back east.

I pull the envelope from my pocket and shuffle through the pictures, studying the faces of these people, these lives that have somehow infected mine. Here's my grandfather, the righteous patriarch, a man who would use racial slurs at the slightest provocation. Here's Uncle William, police officer for fifty-one years, an activist against unionization throughout the Midwest. Here's my cousin from Arkansas, the one relative my family thinks of as having *made it*. She's currently head lackey for a Republican senator, the man pushing for machine-gun nests along the Texas border.

I flip through a few more photos, take a few more sips, so depressed I feel my breathing become labored.

I'm about to put them inside their envelope when I come across a picture I've seen countless times. It's the one of Aunt Janet and the lake, she in her bathing suit, glancing to her left. But what I haven't seen before is my mother sitting beside her, likewise in swimsuit, her child's head thrown backward and her throat exposed. Apparently, this is how the photograph looked before my mother had it cropped. My mother who's never been to this lake, my mother who believes those lying are in danger of hellfire. I can't accept it is really her. Clearly it is—her features, her teeth, her hair smooth and wet—though I have a difficult time recognizing her appearance—hers or my aunt's, either one. It has little to do with context, the oddness of seeing this picture smaller, held in a hand, very little to do with studying the portrait as it was meant to be seen, two children arm in arm, enjoying the weather, the promise of youth. What makes them difficult to distinguish is their eyes or, more precisely, their lack of eyes—these thin-shouldered farm girls, expressions frozen in a laugh—the fact that across the eyes of Janet and my mother, someone has drawn a heavy, dark line, scribbled athwart their temples a blindfold of permanent black.

LARGE OAKS AND CEDARS stand on either side of the road. The morning sun filters through them, their limbs casting wild-patterned shadows along the pavement. From time to time I look away from the blacktop and over at Mother sitting beside me, thumbing the pages of her Sunday school lesson, pages of her Bible. Light and shadow strobe her face and her complexion seems to alter between the two, between leaf shade and sunlight. I attempt for several moments to secure it in my mind the way she actually looks. I've studied her all my life and should be able to conjure something, but the shadows are coming so swiftly that as soon as an image appears, the darkness blurs it. I try slowing the car, speeding up, but the effect is much the same: mother's face flickering and odd.

We emerge from the trees, make it on to the highway, and in several minutes are pulling into the church's gravel parking lot. FIRST PENTECOSTAL, the sign says. VISITORS WELCOME. I find a place close to the front and we enter the sanctuary, sit at the back watching people file in. Mother waves to each, beaming, this morning, to have her prodigal son beside her. Some walk over to greet us, but others simply go to their seats, the same ones, I assume, as the week before. When the room fills and the hands of the clock move to nine thirty-five, the man who performed Kenneth's funeral approaches the pulpit.

In several minutes we are singing. I don't know the words, so my eyes shift between the hymnal and the backs of people's heads, the minister above us belting out the song. By the time we reach the second verse, I've given over the pretense altogether, having become a mere spectator. I hear Mother's voice beside me, so foreign-sounding that I glance at her mouth, *possession* describing this much better than I'd thought. When she catches me looking, she turns toward me slightly, grins.

It was the day before yesterday I found the pictures, and still I haven't spoken of them. Finally, what is there to say? Ask my mother what happened to her at the lake, why her sister committed suicide, the reason she avoided Kenneth all those years? Or perhaps I should suggest she go into counseling, tell her religion is, as Marx said, an opiate to prevent her from facing reality. Finding my place in the songbook, I shake my head at such thoughts and mouth a few words, begin searching to find the chorus.

When it's turned over in my head, I know very little, just segments of a story that barely connect. I can conjecture all I want about Kenneth's motives for giving me his truck, surmise that he did so as confession or payment, a last effort at retribution. Or I could decide it was all intended, that my family's notion of a cartoon devil is not so wide of the mark. But whatever my hypothesis, the pieces of this narrative don't exactly fit, and finally, I'm not sure if I want them to, if I could handle it if they did. After all, as a means of coping, understanding is greatly overrated. There has to be, I think, a better way of dealing with such things, a better way of growing numb. It's hard not to look around me and see that these people have found theirs. Heading toward the final verse, I hear my mother's strong, clear voice, and I know what's just beneath those syllables, know also that they cause her to feel it less. That, I suppose, is something of an accomplishment: finding a cure you can live with, one that doesn't gnaw away at your soul.

After all, there's pain of my own I'd like to assuage. After Father died, I thought education would expand my consciousness, give me a means of comprehending my grief. But, in many respects, it only clouded my awareness all the more. I'll never know the simple abandon I see in my mother, her head tilted and her hands raised, a look on her face as of total assurance. No doubt these people are deluded, their worship little more than a drug. But were it possible, if I could allow my mind to stop churning, it's one I'd consume without hesitation—open my arm to the needle, widen my mouth for the eyedropper or pill. There are even times when I'm convinced I could accept the brainwashing gladly. Provided, of course, it would stand between my eyes and the blindfold, the descending strip of black that, as the years progress, threatens to turn my vision to darkness.

IN TONGUES

He shall wear them when he ministers, and their sound shall be heard when he goes into the holy place before the Lord, and his sons shall wear them when they come near the altar to minister in the holy place, or they will bring guilt on themselves, and die.

—EXODUS 28:35, 43

REVEREND HASSLER WAS a plump man, his hair just graying around the ears, his eyes kind and sad behind thick glasses. By no means common, Hassler was one who possessed what older generations call the gift of tongues. Since the age of twelve the Spirit had come upon him daily, and in the afternoons when he knelt at his couch, a peculiar speech would stammer from his lips.

Hassler began preaching at sixteen and by twenty-one had evangelized across Oklahoma, Arkansas, and much of Missouri. After a nervous breakdown one summer, he spent time in a hospital and then, in the early seventies, settled in Perser, married Anita Etheridge, and began pastoring a rural holiness church.

The First Pentecostal was not large—150 when the sanctuary was filled on Easters—but Hassler's congregation adored him. He stood at the pulpit on Sundays and Wednesday evenings, fervent, effusive, and strangely animate. In either pocket he carried a handkerchief to wipe the sweat from his brow, and often, in the middle of a sentence on Jeremiah or an admonition to repentance, Hassler would begin to speak in the tongues of angels.

It was after just such a night that he awoke and found his gift gone. There was no warning, nor did there seem to be cause. He'd come in the afternoon, knelt in his study, and heard his voice ascend in plain and unbroken English. He remained on his knees till the light grew red in the west window, then rose and walked to the parsonage across the lawn.

At first, this change did not trouble him. Over the years he'd become very content. He knew such things were governed by God, not man, and that the Spirit could not be forced. He did not attempt to compel the tongues, and when his wife asked him what was the matter, he did not mention their ceasing.

Then a week went past, a dry month following. Hassler began to grow anxious, and lying in bed one night, he convinced his wife that they needed to cleanse their home so the Spirit might return.

They took their television to Perser Gun and Pawn, their radio and record player, their collection of blue-grass albums. Hassler persuaded Anita to throw away her drawers of costume jewelry, and himself took his silver-and-turquoise belt buckle and the matching pocket watch and pitched them in the burn barrel.

In two weeks they'd rid their home of magazines, knickknacks, and sugared confections: chocolate and coffee, iced tea and cocoa, the tin of caramel corn neighbors had sent the past Christmas. One evening Hassler went out to his pickup, scratched up the ends of the pinstriping with his pocketknife, and stripped it from the sides of his bed and cab.

Yet, for all this, for all Hassler's supplication, his willingness to divest himself of material possessions, when he knelt at his couch to pray, his speech remained in an earthly tongue.

The weather became hot and dry, and the local paper cautioned residents not to throw cigarettes out their car windows. Hassler walked through his days with an uneasy look, perpetually casting his eyes as if searching for a message in the clouds, a face in the wood paneling to pronounce his deliverance. It was along this time that news came of Leslie Snodgrass.

Snodgrass was an evangelist of fifteen, but everyone who saw him said that being in the presence of the Baptist himself could not have been more remarkable. They told how the boy laid hands on the sick, preached Christ and fire, gave tongues and interpretation both. All believed he was anointed, and when Hassler heard of this, he knew if anyone could help him recover his gift, this boy was he.

He contacted the evangelist's pastor, a Brother Danforth of Tishomingo, and arranged for Snodgrass to hold a revival at the First Pentecostal for as long as he wished. Danforth said Hassler and his congregation were in for a treat.

"You wouldn't believe how God blesses that boy," Danforth told him.

"I don't doubt it," said Hassler, scrawling the word *revival* in enormous letters across the following week of his calendar.

SNODGRASS ARRIVED a few evenings later with a duffel in either hand. He was skinny and very pale. He stood on the green plastic turf of Hassler's front porch and rang the doorbell, an older woman waving to him from the golden LTD he'd just climbed out of.

Hassler and his wife greeted the boy and brought him into the living room. They had always been told their home was inviting, but Snodgrass appeared as if he'd stepped into another world. He stood looking at the indentations in the carpet where the television and stereo had formerly sat, then studied the matching recliners and ceiling fan, the walls where wildflowers hung in imitation brass frames. Finally, he glanced toward the dining room. Ringed by wicker chairs, the glass table was set with bowls of mashed potatoes, green beans, corn. A pork roast rested in the center on a ceramic platter.

The boy turned to them. "Your house is nice," he said.

Hassler looked out his screen door to where the automobile was making a three-point turn. He gestured toward it and asked Snodgrass whether his mother was coming in.

"Grandmother," the boy corrected. "She has a room ready for her at the Fairmont."

The Hasslers looked briefly toward each other; this particular hotel was less than a mile's distance.

"But *you're* staying with us, aren't you?" Anita asked.

"Yes ma'am."

"We have plenty of space," Hassler began to object, rushing at the door to see the gold car pull back onto the highway and remove itself from view. "The bed in the guest room's a queen. She could have slept in there with you or out here on the—"

"Nana wanted it this way," Snodgrass explained. "She said if I'm going to evangelize, I need to learn how to stay with people. She said she won't be around forever."

The Hasslers, forcing oddly identical grins onto

their faces, told him they understood, that his grandmother seemed to have given sound advice.

They made small talk for a while longer, and then Anita ushered Snodgrass and her husband to the table. The plates rested on place mats imprinted with corn of all sizes. The handles of the forks and spoons were plastic cornstalks, and there was corn on the salt and pepper shakers as well. Anita saw the boy examining all of this and laughed nervously.

"I collect corn," she told him. "Anything with corn."

Snodgrass smiled, pulled back a chair.

Hassler said grace, and the three of them ate without exchange, no sounds but the scraping of their forks. He observed the evangelist from the corners of his eyes. He looked frail, Hassler thought, almost elderly. His eyes were darkly circled, the whites slightly pink, and seeing this, Hassler decided there was something otherworldly about him.

When he could no longer bear the silence, the pastor wiped his mouth and pointed to a scar that ran just above the knuckle of the boy's left index finger.

"Where'd that come from?" he asked.

Snodgrass looked at the scar for a moment, then at Hassler.

"Go-cart," he said.

"*Go*-cart?"

"Yes sir. A friend and I were riding go-carts in the pasture a few years back. The chain came loose and cut off my finger."

"Clean off?" Hassler asked.

"It was dangling by skin," Snodgrass told him, and took a long drink of water.

Hassler winced, shook his head in sympathy, but could think of nothing further to say. He found this strange, for he was comfortable with others and could easily draw conversation from them. He looked at his wife, and she began to provoke what discussion she could. But the boy would speak only to answer questions or express gratitude when a dish was passed. After he'd finished eating, he told Anita that dinner was very good and thanked them both.

They rose, sat a few uncomfortable hours in the living room, and then Hassler showed Snodgrass the guest room. He stood in the doorway watching the boy unpack his things, set them in neat rows on the mahogany dresser. The pastor asked if there was anything he needed, if the room was all right, if the bed would be comfortable to sleep on.

Snodgrass smiled. He looked about embarrassedly. "This," he said, faltering, "is the first night I've spent away from home."

"Is that right?"

"Yes sir."

Hassler stood there, not knowing what to say.

"Would it be okay if I slept on the couch?"

"Of course," the pastor told him, "wherever you're—"

"Are you sure?"

"Absolutely. Whatever makes you comfortable."

He helped the boy carry his bedding to the living room, wished him good night, told him if he needed anything to come and wake him. Snodgrass thanked him and Hassler went back down the hallway.

He closed the door to their bedroom, pulled off his trousers and socks, climbed in between the covers. Anita was there waiting. She turned off the light and scooted across the bed toward him.

"What do you think?" she whispered.

"About what?"

"Our evangelist. What do you think about Leslie?"

"He seems like a very sweet boy."

"You think he'll make it a week?"

There was silence and then the sound of Hassler exhaling a long breath.

"Be lucky," he told her, "if he makes it through the night."

REVIVAL BEGAN THE following evening. Hassler and Snodgrass stood in the foyer greeting people as they entered—the pastor warm and affable, the evangelist quiet and tense, utterly out of place. It was a Tuesday, and there was not a large crowd, only a third of the congregation in attendance. At five after, they closed the doors and came down the center aisle. They stepped onto the platform, crossed it, and sat on pew at the auditorium's rear wall— the boy very straight in his dark brown suit, the tips of his loafers just brushing the ground. His grand-mother had taken a position at the front—a small, virtually wrinkleless woman, with a long-sleeved dress and hair woven into a great gray bun. She looked fa-miliar to Hassler, but the preacher could not reckon how. He'd seen a thousand Pentecostal matrons in his time, but none quite as statuesque, none with an ex-pression denoting greater purpose or will.

As people took their seats, Hassler noticed Snod-grass surveying the inside of the building. The sanc-tuary was done up in burgundy: burgundy carpet and pew cushions and great burgundy drapes over the windows. The walls were wood-paneled, matching the altars in color and grain. A piano stood on one side of the platform, an organ on the other, the enor-mous oak podium resting center stage. They had con-structed the new building only a few years before, the money donated by Hassler's uncle, a horse rancher prominent in that area.

Snodgrass told the pastor he had a beautiful church, and Hassler gave him an uneasy smile, wondering if the boy would be able to step behind the podium when the time came.

In a few minutes, Hassler rose from the pew, ap-proached the pulpit, and began the service. There was song and offering; there was prayer request and testimony. Jimmy Osage and his wife sang a special with Carol Fortner playing accompaniment.

At forty-five minutes in, Hassler introduced Snod-grass, and the boy moved toward the pulpit. Hassler went back to his seat, watched the evangelist greet the audience and ask them to bow their heads in prayer. The pastor, nodding in feigned compliance, saw Snodgrass's grandmother press the record button on the tape player she'd brought, noted also that her grandson placed his hands below the podium to conceal their shaking. Hassler closed his eyes, praying that Snodgrass would be able to make it through his sermon.

Then the boy raised his head and began to preach. His tone grew firm, and he spoke in a voice biblical and commanding. Indeed, it seemed as if it was not he who was speaking at all. Hassler sat incredulous, as did the audience. The boy's sermon was an urgent cadence, a voice almost in song, and Hassler knew it was neither affected nor rehearsed. He felt relieved beyond comparison, both for his congregation and himself, assured that the evangelist could be the one to help restore his gift.

As Snodgrass preached, the sincerity of his words cut his audience to the quick, for listening to the boy minister was like hearing a prophetic utterance, and those who had begun to doubt the very truth of God were shaken to their foundations. Elders who had been close to mute shouted amens, the younger and more demonstrative among them stricken dumb. The longer the sermon, the less his audience could wait to fall into the altars, and when this happened, Hassler found himself among them, kneeling in their midst like the commonest reprobate. All around him the congregation cried out to God in voices loud with shame.

Bent over the altar, his eyes tightly clenched, Hassler tried to summon the Spirit. In former days it took very little coaxing. It seemed that when he closed his eyes, there would be a mist waiting just above him and all he had to do was inhale. His face would grow hot and wet, his hands would tremble, and soon his tongue would be released. It was like being emptied of all need for life, and if he could have lived and died that way, he would have.

Now, Hassler struggled among the voices to his right and left, feeling that just beyond the black screen covering his eyes there was something pressing toward him, putting forth impressions as through a bolt of velvet. Whether a face or other shape he could not tell, though there was nothing he would not have forfeited to learn.

But this night, Hassler could not tear aside the veil. He made steady appeal, pleaded, spoke promises. He tried to recall images of himself ten and twenty and thirty years previous, tried to remember the precise feel of the language that had possessed him, the shape of its vowels. He even thought that if he began speaking, began mimicking the voice, perhaps it would return.

Yet, as his congregation began to stand and approach their pews, Hassler realized the Spirit would not come. He rose and returned to his seat, trying to fend away thoughts of desertion.

Anita was sitting there wiping mascara from her eyes. After a while, she placed her head on her husband's shoulder.

"Bobby," she whispered, "this is what we've needed."

He looked at her, then to where the evangelist knelt just to the left of the platform, the boy's face uplifted, his lips stammering.

WORD OF SNODGRASS quickly spread. In three days time numbers at the First Pentecostal swelled to over two hundred, and Hassler was forced to borrow folding chairs from the Assembly of God down the road. People came from far away as Okemah, Guthrie—one family from western Arkansas—all saying it was a true revival. Folks were saved and filled, and there was even talk of using Pete Cochran's pond for a baptism. Night after night, Hassler sat watching the evangelist, wondering what would become of his soul.

It did not seem long since he had been the young man, full of fire and conviction, and during those days he did not think it could be otherwise. Before he could drive, his uncle Jess would take him from church to church to hold revivals or single-night meetings. Neither of his parents would darken a sanctuary's door: his father was bad to drink, his mother dead at forty.

Jess drove into town every afternoon to take his nephew fishing or for ice cream or to church. Having no children of their own, he and his wife all but adopted the boy, and after his sister died, they moved him into their guest room.

Hassler could remember sitting between his aunt and uncle in their step-side Buick, watching the fields scroll past. Jess was a tall man with a sculpted face, Lorraine his physical opposite; in the early twenties they were converted when Pentecost swept the Midwest. He had no call upon him, but in her younger days Lorraine had been an evangelist and even now possessed the gift of prophecy.

During prayer meeting one night—Hassler would have been about eleven—Lorraine began to prophesy over the boy. The woman held his head to her breast and told how God had placed a great anointing on his life, how He had things in store for him the like of which Hassler could never imagine. She said he would grow to be mighty in the Spirit, would evangelize and pastor a church, would lead many toward the path of righteousness. She said that as long as he kept his eyes fixed on his calling, his way would be certain. Lying in bed, Hassler would repeat the prophecy, picturing the face of his mother as he mouthed the words.

The next summer he was baptized in the Holy Ghost with the evidence of speaking in tongues. Until then, Hassler had been possessed of a longing and an emptiness. As a child, he would watch the evenings come with a feeling that someone had thrown a blanket over the face of the world. But when the Spirit descended and the tongues began, Hassler knew that something had altered in the very pit of him. It was as if the part that sought consolation, the thing that needed peace and reassurance, had been covered with a soft, thick material. Not that it had been excised; Hassler was certain it had not. It had merely been covered, wrapped like a ball of spiders into a velvet sack.

Hassler began preaching several years after. It was not the matter of preparation and nerves he thought it would be. He took to it naturally and what he had to say fell from him with the same ease that sweat fell from his brow. All said he was under the sincere anointing of God.

Years passed and Hassler grew both in reputation and confidence. Then one night—Hassler had been holding a three-week revival in Little Rock—Jess and Lorraine received a call. Their nephew was weeping, had been for two days straight.

Jess drove to Arkansas and retrieved the young

man—he sat in the front seat nearly catatonic—and the next week was forced to take him to a psychiatric hospital in Norman. The doctors said Hassler was suffering from a psychosis they hoped would soon disappear.

Hassler never understood what had happened. And in three months time he felt as good as he ever had, the breakdown seeming like a largely jumbled dream. All he remembered was that he had stepped into the pulpit one night, felt the presence of God, and then began to weep. He could not stop to deliver his sermon, nor could he cease when bedtime came, and the following morning when the pastor checked on him, Hassler was weeping yet.

He would later speak about this to his aunt Lorraine. On a late August evening, several years after the occurrence, the two of them sat on the back porch of the ranch house looking out into the woods. It was hot and very dry, and as they spoke the cicadas swelled up in the bushes around them, then went suddenly still.

Hassler leaned into the cane chair and looked at his aunt. She was in her seventies, but did not look it. She was a small woman with doll-like features and clean blue eyes. Lorraine had been talking for half an hour, telling him he had nothing to be ashamed of, that the Spirit of the Lord was a comfort, but the anointing hard to bear.

"I can remember times I'd step into the pulpit,"

his aunt told him. "I'd have a sweat break out on me and feel like my legs were going to buckle."

Hassler smiled.

"I'd get a feeling like I wanted to run, and then another because I knew I couldn't."

Hassler moved forward in his chair. He saw a squirrel run the trunk of a black oak and sit with its tail twittering.

"It's not that I was nervous," he said. "It was more like when you know it's going to storm."

Lorraine began to shake her head. "I never said it had anything to do with *nervous.*"

Hassler gave her a puzzled look, and she raised a hand to her mouth, kept it there a moment, then glanced toward nothing.

"In the Old Testament," she began, "the temple priests sewed bells on their hems. They tied ropes to their ankles. They did this because they were the only ones who could walk behind the curtain. If there was sin on them, God would strike them where they stood; people would drag them out by their ropes."

Hassler nodded.

"I'd be in church, Bobby, waiting to get behind that pulpit, and I'd think how the priests walked past the curtain knowing this. They knew if the sacrifice wasn't pure, the bells would stop. It must have sobered them. It must have made them wish they were never called."

The woman quit speaking and cleared her throat. Hassler began to study the ground.

"I know there's some," Lorraine continued, "who've never felt the anointing, so they wouldn't understand—those people on Christian television prancing around like a carnival. But those who have felt it, they never step on the platform lightly." The woman put a hand on his arm. "Do you know what I'm talking about?"

"I do," said Hassler. "But I don't see it that way."

"Which way?"

"We're not under the Old Law. We're not sacrificing for our—"

"Bobby," said the woman, "you can't tell me that even on the best nights you don't feel it—like you're facing something that could turn on you."

"Of course I feel it," Hassler told her. "I never step behind the podium but what I don't feel it. That's some of the problem. It shouldn't be that way. The Lord shouldn't—"

"You think arguing with it is going to help?"

"You know I don't."

"It's going to make you crazy, is what it'll do. What you have to decide is if it's worth it."

"I don't have a choice," he said.

"Hush now," she told him, "Everyone has a choice. Just because you have a calling doesn't mean you have to answer. Maybe you'll have to tell the Lord no."

Hassler sat for a while. The sun had gone down, casting the yard in darkness. "I can't do that," he finally said.

Lorraine patted him on the arm and pulled her hand away. She seemed to be speaking to herself. "For the person who can receive," she told him, "the Spirit of the Lord and the Spirit of the Devil run alongside, and if a man isn't careful, if he doesn't respect his calling over its signs, he'll pick wrong every time. I've seen it burn people alive."

Hassler noticed it had become quiet. He could hear whippoorwills crying to each other and, from some distance, the knocking of woodpeckers. He eyed his feet and his voice surprised him when it came. "There are times," he said, "I think it's going to kill me."

His aunt drew her arms up to her as if she were unexpectedly cold, and both sat watching the sky darken. It seemed a long time before she spoke.

"I always felt like that in the presence of the Lord," she told him. "Part of me glad of the anointing. Part of me waiting for the bells to stop."

THE REVIVAL ENTERED its third week, and Hassler became ill in both body and mind. Over the past fifteen days, he had seen signs and wonders, salvations and healings, slayings in the Spirit. He had seen people run the aisles and people lie in the floor trembling and people walking the backs of pews. Just a few evenings before, he watched an elderly man fall to the carpet and die, taken in an instant to his reward.

But Hassler remained without blessing. He remained dry as a bone.

The pastor would sit late into the night, flipping determinedly through his Bible. The pages were dog-eared and crumpled—most of the passages underlined in various colors of ink. He read about the kingdom of Heaven suffering violence, about Jacob wrestling with the Lord, about Abraham's dispute with God. Hassler began to see these as precedents. Perhaps, he thought, this was a trial.

He watched Snodgrass very closely, the way the boy approached the pulpit, the way he knelt and prayed. Hassler saw that there was no concern over whether the Spirit would come when called on; the boy would as soon believe there would not be oxygen when he drew his breath. Snodgrass came toward the altar gracefully and with a look of obedience, the doomed look of the terminally ill.

Hassler would lie in bed at night going over these things till his mind was tired and hazed, and he seemed very close to breaking. Whenever he considered that the revival could only last so long, he felt as if someone had placed an iron on his chest. He knew he'd a dwindling number of opportunities to embrace the Spirit, and each evening he forced all his energy toward regaining his gift. He sat with his mind straining toward it, every thought a supplication.

Finally, his thoughts began to turn darker, and he reckoned ways to bring the revival to a close. He could no longer sit watching the Spirit descend on all but him. But when he spoke to his deacons, each responded that to end the revival in such a state would be tantamount to blasphemy. One did not, Emmanuel Beauford reminded him, simply put an end to God's workings. Indeed, Beauford and the evangelist's grandmother had already found themselves of one mind regarding this; she'd called and spoken to him of the matter several nights before. Grudgingly, the pastor agreed, replacing the receiver in its cradle, staring at the floor.

It had been close to a week since Hassler had slept. His mind was blurred, his vision grainy. Out of the corners of his eyes, shapeless shadows jerked and shifted, and when his wife touched him at breakfast one morning, he started as if bitten by a snake.

"Bobby," she said, "what's wrong with you?"

Hassler smoothed both hands over his face, held them at his temples. He rose from the table and went into the bathroom, locking the door behind him.

THAT EVENING THE revival reached a pitch not even the elders could recall. So strongly did they feel the presence of God that the song service was interrupted by preaching, the preaching by a rush to the altars. People could not wait, and they needed neither hymn nor sermon to persuade them.

Hassler looked around the room, seeing that all— they had counted attendance at 227—had joined the evangelist in prayer. They knelt at the altars, and where they'd formerly sat, and some sprawled on the carpet. A commotion arose, cries of remorse and appeal and thanksgiving. There were people standing and some bent double, some with hands uplifted and others holding theirs clasped to the backs of their heads. A great number, men and women alike, were speaking in tongues.

Hassler watched all of this, and there was such longing in him that he had to lower his eyes. He heard the various voices—some fast and loud, some slow, and rhythmic, and melodious. His stomach turned and his heart drummed harsh, tinny as a snare.

He sat for a while, trying to count himself fortunate, thinking that, after all, his material needs were provided for: he had a wife and a congregation who loved him; he was doing what he had been told was his calling. There were very few, he thought, who made it so far.

He closed his eyes, tilted his head, and attempted to express gratitude. But as he did this, the fluorescent light filtering his lids caused the darkness to take a reddish tint. It seemed he was trying to peer through a thin veil, one so frail it could be torn away with no effort at all.

He thought of those Scriptures he'd recently read, passages dictating that he who wanted a blessing must surely demand it. The curtain of the Old Covenant was thick, accessible to few. Christ, he thought, had thinned it, made it the consistency of paper. He had thinned it and placed within each the agency to tear it to shreds.

Hassler began to grow eager; this was the end of his trial. God Almighty was instructing him in the ways of a new covenant. All these months he had been approaching the restoration of his gift like one unfamiliar with the things of the Spirit. He had, he decided, been a fool.

Hassler looked down from the platform. The congregation was still around the altars; not even the musicians had stood to perform hymns, as they were accustomed to at this point in the service. Often, Hassler would lead them. After communing with the Spirit, he took great pleasure in standing there emptied, providing music for those who still prayed.

It occurred to him that if he were to approach the pulpit and begin singing, this would compel the tongues. He could even begin speaking, forming random words, and if he made such a step, surely God would transform this into heavenly speech.

Hassler rose from his seat, went down from the platform to where the pianist knelt, tapped on her shoulder, and motioned her to the stage. The woman wiped her face, stood, and obediently walked to the piano, weaving her way among the kneeling bodies. Hassler followed, and soon found himself behind the podium. He looked at Carol.

" 'Blessed Assurance,' " he told her. "Key of E-flat."

The woman began to play, Hassler to sing, and they made it through the first and second verse, the chorus. They finished the song and started another. The congregation did not seem to notice; each was in a different state of meditation or repentance or blessing.

When they came to the bridge, Hassler gripped the edges of the podium in either hand, leaned against it, and shut his eyes.

His thought was simply to begin speaking—anything that might sound like tongues. He would not scrutinize the syllables or their effect; he would speak out of faith and await his voice's conversion. As he heard the song turn once again toward the verse, Hassler opened his mouth, paused for a moment, and began. He did not consider his words. He stood with eyes shut, forcing his speech into the light beyond.

AT SOME POINT, Hassler was aware the music had stopped. He could not remember it having happened and wondered how much time had passed. He opened his eyes, then lowered them to the altars. His congregation was still there, but there were none praying. They were silent and perfectly still, each casting him a curious expression. Snodgrass knelt in their midst with a fitful look on his face. The boy appeared to be witnessing a slaughter.

Hassler stepped away from the podium. It was only then that he realized his lips were still moving, an unassisted speech leaving his mouth. But this was not the speech that Hassler had begun to speak moments before in the hopes that God would transform it. Nor was it the one he had known most his life, the vowels that had come upon him at the age of twelve. This language was guttural and hard, slightly metallic. It was abrasive, a fast and repetitive cough.

The pastor tried to shut his mouth, but he could not. He clenched his jaw and pressed his tongue against his palate, but the words came regardless. Catching his tongue between his teeth, he held it there, but it came loose and flapped inside his mouth like an ailing bird. Hassler began to tremble and his mind rushed all directions. He looked at the ceiling and he looked at the floor, and he shut his eyes to bring darkness to them. He did this to restore the veil, but there was no veil, and even with his eyes clenched the room seemed very bright. Everywhere the light poured. His eyes were full of it, his ears loud with the unclean speech.

Hassler moved off the platform and walked toward his congregation. People rose, backed away.

He walked before them like an infant, and there was part of his mind that spoke this foul tongue and part that watched it speak. The latter wanted very badly to tell them something, particularly the boy who still knelt at the altars, frozen on his knees in an attitude of panic. But Hassler could not remember what he wanted to tell them, and he could not make his tongue comply with his wishes. His glance swept briefly over the evangelist's grandmother, on whose face he seemed to detect the creases of a grin.

As the deacons came forward, trying to escort him out the back, Hassler fixed his eyes on Snodgrass. The two of them shared a look, but no one could tell whether there was understanding between them. The men continued walking their preacher toward the door, calmly, as if ushering a drunk. Hassler stumbled between them, still mouthing the unfamiliar speech. And yet, by the time he reached the parking lot, he no longer heard it. Neither did he hear the cicadas nor the two men pacing beside him. Hassler heard nothing, and as his deacons assisted him into the backseat of a car, he grew dizzy and again closed his eyes: one man pushing gently at his right, the other on the opposite side of the vehicle, leaning inside and over the seat, tugging his pastor slowly across. Hassler lost all sense of whereabouts, pulled gradually, though he did not know how — perhaps by means of a rope. The preacher was certain his deacons had heard, the silence unmistakable, not so much a void of sound but a quiet with its own distinct tenor, a vibration that rang noiselessly in his ears, indicating to those outside that the bells had stopped.

THE BACKSLIDERS

SHOULDERING HIS DUFFEL and a large canvas sack, the boy stepped out onto the porch of his grandfather's trailer, knuckling sleep from his eyes' corners, glancing about in the predawn. The sky was just gathering in the east, shades of rose and crimson, and the oaks surrounding the residence stood blurred against it. As Jonathan watched, they began slowly to articulate: trunks and limbs and then smaller branches, individual leaves, their edges downturned and crumpled. At the barbed-wire fence marking the property line was a large elm, and the boy looked for, then found, the swollen knot that had over the years grown around the fence's top strand. He'd wondered over this phenomenon with a sick feeling, curiosity and an attendant revulsion, as he tugged the rusted wire emerging from either end of the gnarl. One afternoon, he went to attack the eyesore with cable cutters, but his grandfather found him at the task and warned him away with a switch. Now Jonathan observed the tree from a distance, impatient to understand how such an oddity might be allowed.

He was a stocky child—ten years of age, black hair, arms dark from a summer of fishing. In many respects, he looked a miniaturized opposite of his grandfather, Emmanuel Beauford, local rancher and deacon of the First Pentecostal. Beauford was thin and well built, angular, his skin drawn tightly across his skull. Seen in a proper light, the man's face appeared almost skeletal, his eyes deep-set, alert. While the sternness of younger days had faded somewhat, he remained, nonetheless, determined, committed to his notions of holiness. Jonathan would often beg to stay with Beauford on weekends, and on occasion the man would awaken to find his grandson gone from the pallet he'd made him, curled at the side of his bed. Removing the quilts, Beauford would kneel on the floor, work his hands under the boy's torso, and lift him to the mattress.

This morning, Beauford had roused his grandson early, for they were to meet a group of men in the woods five miles south; Jonathan had been allowed to invite a few of his friends as well. Jude McCoin, a fellow deacon, had been diagnosed with esophageal cancer, and though their church had been in revival for over two months, his condition had grown steadily worse. Led by Beauford, the men had decided a retreat was in order, that worshiping in a mixed congregation prevented the deacon from being restored. Jonathan had heard his grandfather say that a man was never so close to God than when alone with his brethren, away from the impurities of the rival gender.

"It is women," he'd pronounced the Sunday previous, "that permit the Devil to work." He cleared his throat, proceeded in a somber tone. "I'm not talking about a godly woman like Sister Snodgrass who submits herself to the sanctity of Christ. I'm talking about the other kind: those who confess to giving over their hearts and then reserve a portion of it for the flesh. It is a thing Paul brings before us time and again: the carnal nature of the female. Whether they intend it or they don't—in God's mind, it does not matter." Pausing, he lent each man a look, swept his eyes over the three boys who were sitting with them in the fellowship hall. "You take what they bring of the luxuries, their hair combing and prancing in the mirror—you take that away and you'll have given the Spirit room to work."

Pete Cochran, a disciple of Beauford's since the early sixties, affirmed this, looking toward the others to read their opinion. They—Jim Fortner and

Thomas Riley, Lucas Kesterson and Timothy Sweet
—were also in agreement.

"So," Beauford continued, "we go out to the camp
and settle in, get down to business. I mean *really* down
to business—not sit around the fire visiting. We do
that, we might see Jude beat this thing." Beauford
tightened his mouth, gave a series of nods. "I believe
that," he said, pressing his hands together. "I believe
the Lord will spare him."

Jonathan glanced at McCoin a few chairs away—
his frail-looking neck, his eyes magnified by thick
lenses. It seemed McCoin was less enthusiastic than
his companions, as if, though he raised no objection
to the outing, he would've much preferred staying
behind. This bothered Jonathan, for he was moved
by his grandfather's words and could see his grandfather was also moved when he'd spoken them. He
studied the thin sprawl of hair atop McCoin's head,
the ashen look of his skin, angry that the man was
not properly grateful for what his grandfather was
trying to accomplish. He grew so absorbed in these
thoughts that he failed for a moment to perceive the
deacon had become aware of his being observed.

Jerking his eyes to the floor, Jonathan steered them
about the room, returning warily to McCoin's face.
The man was looking directly at him. Crossing one
leg over the other, he smiled broadly at the boy and
winked.

THE AREA IN which they made their camp was heavily wooded, and Jonathan had never seen its like—black oaks crowding a steep embankment with a creek running beneath, evergreens on the far side and a hill grown with moss. The men and three boys had hiked for hours under the canopy of leaves, Beauford leading them into denser wood, farther upstream to the hills. Midafternoon, they struck a trail that skirted a series of large boulders and made their way under the high wall of a cliff. There they found a shallow cave of ten or twelve feet into which the boys could walk without stooping. Beauford told the group he'd often camped in the location, and as they looked about they saw a leaf-choked ring of stones, blackened by fire. The others unbuckled their packs, and Cochran began to tell how he and Beauford had used the site as a hunting camp, taking shelter inside when a tornado came through in '68.

The remainder of the day was spent settling in. Kesterson climbed the hill and dug a latrine while the others gathered firewood or spread dried leaves as cushion for their sleeping bags. When evening came they built a fire—the boys roasting franks on hickory spits and the men boiling coffee atop a grate. As it became darker, the elders began to relate stories of their youth, and the boys listened, encouraging them to go on, asking would they repeat certain parts or tell others they'd heard before. Jonathan saw that McCoin sat apart from the rest, sipping into a porcelain mug. He turned at a certain point and caught the man's eyes, red and strange-seeming in the firelight.

The next morning, he awoke at the mouth of the cave and saw that the men were gone. His friends lay on either side of him and he heard voices that he recognized as those of his grandfather and the others. He worked his way out of his sleeping bag and crawled into the light, craning his neck around a corner of rock. On a group of stones just down the path the men sat with Bibles opened on their laps, Beauford leading them in discussion.

Jonathan crawled back into the cave and stared at the two boys in their bedding. He went to the larger of the two, a sandy-haired, obese child, named J.W.— covers thrown off, shirt hiked high on his belly— and began to squeeze his shoulder. The boy's eyelids split slightly and he regarded Jonathan with disdain.

"Whayouwan?"

"Get up," Jonathan told him.

"Why?"

"It's time."

J.W. pulled his shirt down and rolled onto an elbow, shading his eyes with a hand. Jonathan knelt beside him.

"Where's your granddad?" J.W. asked. "Uncle Tim?"

"They're out talking."

"They gonna let us swim?"

"I think so."

"We don't have to pray with them all day?"

Jonathan shook his head. J.W. yawned and looked over to the third boy, nothing visible outside his bedding but a tuft of red hair. He judged where his face should be and delivered a backhand to it. A muffled cry came from the covers and the form inside them composed itself into a ball.

"Scoot," said J.W., delivering a kick. "Get up."

One end of the ball moaned.

J.W. grabbed Scoot's covers, yanked them off, and straddling the thin figure now exposed, began rubbing a knuckle across his scalp. The boy tried to fight off J.W. and then started to scream. Jonathan was pleading with both of them, when his grandfather's face appeared at the mouth of the cave.

"What's wrong with you all?"

Three pairs of eyes stared back at him blankly.

Stooping with his hands on his knees, Beauford delivered an impromptu lecture, telling the boys if they didn't behave, he'd separate them; that they'd not be asked to go camping again; that he'd tell their fathers when he took them home. J.W. climbed off of Scoot and crawled dejectedly toward his sleeping bag. Jonathan looked up at his grandfather.

"Can we swim?" he asked.

"I'd hoped you all might kneel with us awhile. You know how sick Brother Jude is."

Jonathan nodded, and soon the three boys were

sitting cross-legged inside the circle of men, listening as different ones quoted Scripture, extended words of encouragement to their dying companion. McCoin attended to each, periodically nodding, thanking the men for their thoughts. Beauford said they'd done right in coming out to the location, that since the task was laid upon his heart, God's own word proclaimed that as long as they continued in their vigil, McCoin could not help but be delivered. Jonathan considered this, feeling proud of his grandfather. He looked, now and again, at the other boys: Scoot staring open-mouthed at the branches, J.W. digging mud from the grooves of his sneakers with a twig. Jonathan felt contempt for them, wondering how they could be so callous, and when the men kneeled and began their supplications, he joined them, occasionally looking up from between his folded hands to watch the boys snigger quietly to one another.

But after a half hour had passed, his mind too began to wander, and the men—some clustered together making appeals to God, others kneeling a little apart and muttering softly with eyes clenched —showed no signs of ceasing. Finally, he rose to his feet and walked down to the creek where the two boys had snuck away to toss pebbles at crawfish, hands on mouths to suppress their giggling. Glancing anxiously up the hill, Jonathan reluctantly joined them. Little by little, however, he forgot, and after several more minutes—one boy pushed, another pushing back, playful threats, a clump of mud thrown —all three of them were in the stream, splashing and shouting back and forth in shrill voices. They heard, of a sudden, a sharp whistle and, looking up, saw Beauford striding determinedly down the hill. He lifted his grandson from the water, gave him two firm swats on the backside, and told them if all they wanted was to play, they should go farther downstream to do it, to at least have that much respect for the Lord and His work.

J.W. and Scoot walked up onto the bank and stood there quietly dripping while Beauford pulled his grandson aside.

"I don't mind you having fun," he said. "I know you're kids. But I want to say I reckoned a little more from you."

Jonathan looked down at a patch of moss growing on a nearby rock, trying to think of what to say. When it finally came to him and he lifted his head to do so, he saw his grandfather walking back toward the other men, his shirt pulled tight across his shoulder blades, his neck rigid, perfectly straight.

THEY WENT OUT among the blackjacks, shuffling through fallen leaves, ducking the fingers of low-reaching branches. Scoot, younger by several years, would travel a little ahead of the other two, sprinting out in front of Jonathan and J.W., sometimes running back to circle them, his arms spread winglike at his sides, his lips rumbling. Jonathan watched him, looking back, now and then, toward the outcrop of rock where his grandfather and the other men knelt in prayer.

The stream at their left, they crossed a trench of dry and splintered clay, walking until they found an enormous gray sandstone, lichen-covered and worn concave. Scoot ran ahead, jumped, and landing in the stone's center, rolled onto his back and stared at the morning sky.

"The rock is hot," he announced.

Jonathan and J.W. came to either side of him and sat, extending their legs and regarding the patch of azure framed by oak limbs. They started talking of the stories they'd heard the previous night, stories of tornadoes and wildcats and men who'd sought refuge in this region. J.W. claimed that what they had heard was nothing, that the men simply didn't want to scare them, that his uncle had recounted stories better than anything his grandfather had said all evening. He lay over onto his side.

"Uncle Tim told me there were caves down here bigger than even the one we slept in."

"Bigger than last night's?"

J.W. nodded. "He said back in the West days, Jesse James and his gang hid there."

Jonathan gave him a sharp look. "He didn't either."

"He did," J.W. told him.

"Unh-uh."

"You don't believe me?"

"No."

"You calling Uncle Tim a liar?"

"No."

"You calling *me* a liar?"

"Yes," Jonathan said.

"You want to wrestle for it?"

"No."

"All right then."

Scoot rolled onto his stomach and stretched his arms out in front of him. He reached back and lifted his shirt, exposing his skin to the rock.

Jonathan watched this and then, curling his legs, shifted his weight and sat on his ankles. "How do you know Jesse James was there?" he asked.

"They say his name is spray-painted on the walls."

"They didn't have *spray* paint."

"Yes, they did," J.W. told him.

"No, they didn't."

"Carved then."

"Carved where?"

"Carved on the cave wall."

"How far?" Jonathan asked him.

"I bet if we keep going we could find it."

"I bet we get our rears tanned."

"They're supposed to be just downstream."

Jonathan went to ask another question, but Scoot interrupted, wanting he and J.W. to look at something. They looked. The child was still lying on his stomach, but now beamed an expression of complete wonder.

"What is it?" said J.W.

"It's cool," Scoot told him.

Jonathan and J.W. looked at each other. They asked him what he was talking about.

"The rock," Scoot explained. "When we came here it was hot. Now, with me lying on it, it's cool."

They sat staring at him, and then J.W. exhaled slowly, rose to his feet, and began brushing at the backside of his jeans. He looked away toward some hypothetical location.

"Fine," he told Jonathan, already walking, "I'll go look at Jesse's hideout. You can stay here with the professor."

THE BOYS WALKED for what seemed hours, sometimes leaving the stream, sometimes following a path that traveled directly beside it. They made their way through a thicket of briars, over a tumble of rocks, and emerged at last onto the shelf of a vast gorge—flanked on all sides by the green of oak leaves—as if a great hand had reached from the sky and scooped away ten acres of land, leaving behind an enormous brown chasm. The ground dropped sheer at their feet and the stream fell over a sandstone lip to a pool thirty feet below, rushing over a series of falls at the pool's far end. At the bottom, all around the canyon, cave openings pocked the cliff face.

They stood marveling at the discovery—pointing out the various caves they would venture into, hurling rocks at the water below—and then began seeking a way down. Urinating off one of the cliff walls, J.W. found a slope graded just so that they could half slide, half stumble their way to the bottom, and when all three had done this, they crossed the stream on a series of treacherous stones and began making for the entrance to the nearest cave, an opening much wider than it was high. It was barely twenty feet deep, and they came out to explore another, their excitement steadily increasing until they went at a dead run—darting into this cavern to look hastily about, scurrying into another like creatures in pursuit. When Jonathan asked what would happen if they stumbled on a snake, both boys shot him a look. He didn't ask a second time.

The first caves were little but overhangs in the surface of the rock, areas of deep erosion or boulders that had arranged themselves so as to create sandstone shelters. But there were others that went far back into the hillside, narrowing as they went, the light behind them growing ever fainter, even Scoot unwilling to venture further inside. They found the scattered remains of animals, and in one cave they uncovered the entire skeleton of a coyote or fox, half buried in the dirt floor, its bones fragile and thin, as if carved from chalk. J.W. picked up the skull and held it for a moment, then hurled it at the wall: fragments of splintered white and a sharp echo, silence and a brief cloud of dust.

They had surveyed their tenth cave when Jonathan spotted on the far side of the gorge one with a narrower entrance. J.W. panting, wet with perspiration, seated himself on a boulder and told them to go on, that he would catch up in a moment. The two boys made their way quickly across the ravine, Jonathan feeling himself growing winded. He looked at Scoot walking beside him, hoping to see signs of fatigue in him as well, but the only indication of this were a few strands of red hair plastered wetly against his forehead.

Reaching the cave's opening—about man high, three feet in width—Jonathan allowed Scoot to go in ahead. They walked inside, their eyes adjusting to the dim light, and saw that the walls were covered in spray paint—names and figures in palimpsest, numerals anticipating graduation dates, a bizarre mosaic of colors wherein Jonathan could just make out the head of an Indian chief, the town's high school mascot. They saw also that what had seemed to be the cave's rear wall was only a corner. Moving forward, they tracked across a fine dirt the consistency of powder, a floor littered with beer cans, and then, rounding the corner, stood looking into the next chamber. It was darker there, but a shaft of light fell from a crevice high in the ceiling, illuming, to some degree, the sandstone room. They were walking farther in, their eyes still focusing, when they heard a sound—the grunt of what they took to be an animal in pain.

The boys came to a halt, listening as the noise rose steadily in volume. Then, as if snapping from a hazed background into sharper focus, they saw a form struggling on the cave floor, two forms, the shapes shifting in Jonathan's mind from one animal into another—dog to wildcat, coyote to wolf—and then coalescing, finally, into their reality: two men—one on his elbows and knees, the other behind him in a modified kneel. Both were groaning and they faced the same direction, but did not see, for their eyes were clenched. The boys stood watching them, trying to understand what it was they were doing. Something in Jonathan made him lean forward to better view the scene, a simultaneous nausea rising in his stomach, a prickling along the hairs of his arms and neck. He had begun gradually backing from the room when, in front of him, Scoot let out a long, piercing scream.

Then he was running. He did not look back to his friend, and he did not have to, for Scoot quickly passed him, the boy making for the other side of the gorge, his arms and legs a blur. Jonathan's heart pounded and he could hear the wind droning loudly in his ears, the blood rushing in concert there, and looking ahead, saw Scoot pass the rock where J.W. sat, bewildered. Jonathan lowered his head and ran. He could hear shouting from behind him, the voices of men, though he did not understand what those voices said. Passing J.W., Jonathan managed to pant the word *hide.*

Scoot had crossed the stream—splashing through the shallow creek, looking as if he were running on top of the water—and was already scrambling up the hill where they had descended an hour before. Jonathan followed, not seeming to feel his body, only a warm sensation at the crown of his head. When he reached the foot of the hill, looked up to see Scoot attain its summit and disappear from sight, he thought, *I won't be able to climb it; I was barely able to get down.* There followed a distorted period of clambering upward, scraping against rocks, the grasped end of a tree root, and the next thought Jonathan had came to him as he sprinted into the black oaks, dodging trunk and tree limb, hearing shouts in the canyon below.

Scoot was not to be seen. Jonathan continued running but after some time reduced his pace, for all he heard now were the leaves crunching under his feet. He ran slower, and then more slowly, and then was walking, his breath coming to him in gasps. He stopped, finally, and collapsed at the foot of a gnarled pine.

He sat there, trying to calm himself, to convince a

part of his mind that he was safe. His breathing had all but returned to normal when he realized he was not sure in which direction the creek lay, which direction the canyon or camp. He rose and began walking, not recognizing anything he saw. After a while he took another course, and then another. A rush of panic went through him and he began running blindly among the trees. Woods and the occasional clearing went strobing past, each more foreign than the one before it. He entered a sunlit stretch where the oaks thinned and, quickening his pace, felt his foot go down too far into a drift of leaves. His vision seemed to tumble and he fell, skidding several feet on his arm and shoulder. He lay for a few moments with his chest heaving and then grabbed for his ankle. It throbbed, already swelling. Rising up on a knee, he rested his heel on the ground and tried to stand. A tremendous pain shot from the ball of his foot to the shin, and he went to the ground, his vision swarming with translucent specks.

Jonathan rocked back and forth, rubbing his ankle and glancing nervously at the woods around him. He realized he had begun crying but made no effort to wipe his face. Using his uninjured leg, he pushed himself against the trunk of a large oak, and keeping his ankle, as best he could, clear, began to shinny up the tree. The forest floor shrank, and he ascended through branches less and less thick, coming to rest twenty feet from the ground, concealed in the tree's fork. He straddled it, leaned his face and body against the trunk. He was beginning to wonder about J.W. and Scoot when he heard the familiar sound of leaves crunching.

Peering through the limbs, he saw two men walking toward the tree where he was hiding, talking together in hushed tones. One wore a black T-shirt, the other a green pullover. On this jersey was the number twelve, the profiled head of an Indian chief embossed in glittering white.

JONATHAN CLOSED HIS EYES and pressed himself against the tree. He muttered, in his thoughts, snatches of prayers, old hymns, hearing more loudly the voices of the men, the shuffling of leaves. He began making entreaties to a God who, in his imagination, was always a strange amalgam of his grandfather and a face in the clouds, promising renewed dedication, vows of missionary work, physical hardship. He remembered, for some reason, having looked at naked women in a magazine, and he swore he would never again do this, never allow women to take his purity from him, never even take one to wife. He was straining to think of other things he might offer God when he realized that the woods had become silent. Lifting his head slowly from the tree trunk, he looked below him in all directions. The men were gone.

Hours passed, and Jonathan watched the late

summer afternoon fade into evening, a red-and-golden light dyeing the western edges of leaf and limb. All around, the forest took on a hazed look, and he glanced down at his ankle which was red and distended, swollen against his shoe. This was a time of day Jonathan had always feared. His mood seemed to decline with the sun, and now alone, away from home and family, unsure as to what might happen, this feeling was magnified. He thought of the men in the cave, and he hated them for leaving him in the woods alone and injured. And with that surge of hatred, something gave way—a surfeit of emotion, a point of absolute saturation. He lay back against the tree, closed his eyes, and in a few moments was asleep.

He awoke to the sound of someone calling his name. The woods were dim now, but not fully dark, and when he heard the voice again, he did not give a response but began immediately to clamber, descending from limb to limb, sliding along the smooth trunk. When he reached bottom he saw that it was his grandfather who was calling: his grandfather and Jude McCoin, J.W. and his grandfather's friend, Pete Cochran. Cochran led another man by the scruff of the neck—a grasp of bunched fabric as handle—and as they came closer Jonathan saw it was the man with the green jersey, the man from the cave.

Leaning his weight against the tree, Jonathan

shouted to his grandfather. The entire pack moved toward the boy, Beauford running ahead of the others, reaching Jonathan first, picking him up and carrying him some distance, asking, as he carried him, if he was hurt, interspersing his questions with thanksgiving, though to whom this was directed, the boy could not tell. He seated Jonathan on the ground and, kneeling, took him by the shoulders. The old man glanced the boy over, saw that his arms were covered with scrapes, that there was a lengthy scratch along one cheek. He turned his head.

"Pete," he said in an urgent voice, "don't come up here. Keep that nancy back a ways."

Cochran seized a firmer grip on the man he was leading and, pushing him to the ground, knelt with both knees in the small of the man's back. He grabbed a handful of his hair and pressed his face into dirt. "Stay put," he said.

The man muttered something Jonathan could not make out and he saw McCoin walk calmly up and place a hand on Cochran's shoulder. He looked to be reasoning with him, but Jonathan's attention was directed back to his grandfather, his face close to his now, something in his eyes that was utterly foreign.

"Where's Scoot?" asked Jonathan. "Is he all right?"

"He's just fine," the old man whispered. "He's with Brother Tim and the rest. They went around the other way looking for you." Beauford stopped, lowered his head. "They came back and told us what happened, Jon. They came and told us what you saw."

A ruckus had broken out between Cochran and McCoin. The former swore, stood up, and pushed the sick man away. "This ain't none of your business," he told him. "It's between Emmanuel and this—" He trailed off, delivered a kick to the man's side, and climbed back atop him.

"Listen," Jonathan's grandfather said to him, taking the boy's face between his hands, "I want you to tell me the truth. No matter what he did to you, it's not your fault; it won't have even happened. The blood of Christ will *make* it so it will never have happened. He's a devil from Hell, and the Devil's got no power over the children of God. You just tell me, Jon." The man's face seemed to tighten. "You tell me exactly what he did."

Jonathan didn't understand what his grandfather was asking. He opened his mouth to tell about his ankle, how he was running and it went too far into the ground, but instead of speech, there came a sudden burst of sobbing, all the fear and anxiety of the day tumbling out in one confused spasm. He buried his face in his grandfather's chest and felt his big hand cupping the back of his head, stroking it at first, then trembling violently. His grandfather pulled away and looked at Jonathan once more. "That's all

176

right," he said, faltering, his eyes gone strange. "The blood of the Savior will cleanse us both."

Turning, he called to McCoin. "Jude," he said in a commanding tone, "take these boys back to camp. You'll have to carry, Jon. There's something the matter with his leg."

"Emmie," suggested McCoin, "why don't we—"

"Do it," Beauford ordered, rising, walking toward where Cochran knelt on the man's back. Seeing Beauford's approach, Cochran pulled the man upright so that he was genuflecting, his hands, Jonathan noticed, bound by something. McCoin attempted to step in Beauford's path, but the latter pushed him clear, took two more steps, and brought his fist against the captive's face. A spurt of black ejected into the leaves and the man pitched over onto his side. Jonathan saw the man was much younger than he had thought.

Jonathan crawled nearer, toward his grandfather and the young man he now straddled, his grandfather slapping the man's face, asking why he did it, did he know it was an abomination, did he know what they called his kind in Scripture, those who molested children and lay with others of their sex? All this time Cochran argued with McCoin, telling him to take the boys and leave, that they didn't need to witness this. McCoin would not do it: "He's going to kill that kid—don't you see?" Looking over, Jonathan saw J.W. was bent double, vomiting.

177

He had crawled even closer by this point, just five or six feet from where Beauford knelt atop the man, though neither they nor the others were aware of him. The young man was pleading with Beauford: he didn't know what Beauford was talking about; he hadn't hurt anyone; he was wide receiver for the Perser Football team; he'd just turned sixteen. Yes, he and his friend had been fooling around, but they had chased the boys only to scare them.

"Please," he said, mumbling around broken teeth, "we were just afraid they might tell."

"They told," said Beauford, driving his fist once more into the side of the young man's head. His face recoiled from the blow, and his body gave a tremendous jerk, then began to convulse. Beauford rose, startled by this. He looked over to McCoin and Cochran. "He's going into seizure," McCoin warned, and indeed, that looked to be the case, for the young man's body shivered as if wired to a socket. Jonathan watched him, transfixed. He was aware that his crying had stopped, and he wanted the man to stop trembling; it disturbed him the way he moved. But he continued coming closer, wanting to tell the quaking figure that his grandfather was a very strong man, that he was sorry he had hated him, but that now he would know better: he wouldn't chase children and force them to hurt their ankles and to hide, by themselves, in fear for their lives. And with this thought came another, as if traveling alongside and then eclipsing it entirely. He understood, finally, what his grandfather had before been asking, and he began to shake his head, as if the young man's seizures were contagious — shouting *that wasn't what happened, that wasn't it at all*. And just as his protestations became their loudest, the man beside him gave one final shudder and then went still.

McCoin pushed past Cochran, past Beauford who now stood above the young man, staring down at him mutely. He laid his head to the teenager's chest for a full minute and glanced up at Beauford. When he went to speak, no words came from his mouth.

Jonathan had also fallen silent. He sat across from McCoin, realizing, somehow, he'd adopted the same posture — kneeling in the dirt with legs tucked underneath, hunching slightly, arms bracing him at the sides. He looked at McCoin, the man's appearance seeming at once to soften, his features warm and thoughtful in the day's final light. Jonathan shook his head, trying to divest himself of the strange affinity, this sudden sense of kinship. He turned and stared up at Beauford, hoping to find something to contradict these notions, some detail in his grandfather's face in which to confide. But due to the hastening darkness, he could not see the old man's expression, backlit as he was, clouded by night and the forest shade.

DOG ON THE CROSS

———————————

DEPUTY MARTIN DIDN'T want to take the call. It was the hottest summer Oklahoma had seen in two decades, and he wanted to sit in the station with his boots on the desktop, drink coffee, and read *The Perser Chronicle*. For the past three years he'd driven out to every farm and rural residence in the county—domestic disputes and petty vandalism, the more extreme cases involving a stolen tractor or possibly a camper shell. To him, "you'll have to see it to believe it" meant an addled rancher and his hysterical wife, skinny calves hip deep in mud and bawling for their mothers.

This was what he was thinking as he turned off the highway and into the white gravel parking lot of the First Pentecostal, a modest building overlooking a sea of black oak in the valley beneath it. Pulling into a space in front of the church, he put his car in park and switched off the engine. On the steps leading to the main entrance sat Doyle Withers, a dark-complexioned man in dress slacks and a long-sleeved shirt, the collar already damp with sweat. The man was thick jowled and portly; his stomach protruded over his belt. He rose when Martin stepped from his car and tottered over to meet him.

The two exchanged pleasantries and then began walking toward the highway. As they spoke, Martin noticed for the first time the faded green tarp next to the sign at the side of the road. He'd been past the church hundreds of times and it suddenly occurred to him that beside the sign, a small wooden cross was set into the ground, that this was what the tarp had been draped over. When they reached it, Deacon Withers sunk his hands in his pockets and began to rattle change.

"I come out this morning to do the books," he told Martin. "We been in revival about a month now, and this morning I come out and saw it soon as I pulled in. I ran out to the toolshed, got that piece of canvas, and covered it best I could." He paused, coughed into his hand. "Blasphemy is what it is."

Martin reached over, grabbed one corner of the tarp, and tossed it back. Starting, he retreated several steps, looked at the cross and then back to Withers. The deacon had lowered his head.

On the cross was a beagle puppy, a dog of maybe six months. Its forepaws had been secured to the transverse beam by two sixteen-penny nails, its rear legs crossed and nailed through with one. Flies skimmed its muzzle, trailed along the strips of duct tape that held the dog's mouth. From the angle Martin first observed it, the animal looked to be smiling.

The deputy pulled the tarp back over and turned to Withers. His face had a nauseated expression.

"What time you find this?" he asked.

"Earlier this morning. About nine thirty."

"And you called us soon as you saw it?"

"Just the minute I got done with the tarp."

Martin took a small tablet from his pocket, clicked his pen, and went to jot a few notes. His hands, he noticed, were trembling.

"You have any idea who could've done this?"

Withers began to nod, as if he'd meant to tell the deputy but hadn't yet gotten to it.

"I'm about satisfied it was that Hollis fella."

"Who?"

The deacon gestured to the valley below them. "Jacob Hollis. Lives down the hill there."

"Spell his name for me."

"H-o-l-l-i-s. He moved in and built an underground home a few years back. Been after us ever since."

Martin looked up from the tablet. " 'Been after' how?"

"What's that?"

"How's he been bothering you?"

"He comes up every so often and starts raising a commotion, telling us we need to keep it down. Works out of his home, I think. Scientist or something."

"Scientist?"

"I don't know," Withers told him, making vague gestures with his hands. "I think that's what he does. He's about half queer, you ask me. Big ole sucker. Brother Leslie and his grandmother went down and tried to witness to him one afternoon and he told them he was from back east. Said he didn't even believe in God."

Martin wrote steadily for a minute or so, replaced the notepad in his shirt pocket, and buttoned it. The two of them began walking back toward the church.

"You think he's actually capable of this?"

Withers bit his thumbnail and spat. "Yes, I do."

"But you don't really know him?"

"No."

"Ever talked to him?"

Withers shook his head.

"You still think he might've had something to do with it, though."

They had reached the building's front porch. The deacon lowered himself onto a step and hitched his trouser legs.

"I'll put it this way," he said, fixing Martin with

a stare. "It surprises the living daylights out of me he ain't already done a lot worse."

The deputy looked over to the cross. A sudden gust of wind raised one corner of tarp and held it almost vertically, dirt from the side of the road kicking up and spinning across the highway. The wind died and the air once again became hot and still. The angle of canvas lowered back to the ground.

FIFTEEN MINUTES LATER, Martin crossed the churchyard, went over the fence at the turnstile, and started down the hill. He was a tall man and remarkably slender, still a few years shy of forty. His eyes were bright and his nose pointed; his red hair encircled a balding crown. Despite being lanky, he moved with a certain grace, as if each step had been planned long in advance.

Below him lay the valley. Through the limbs of blackjacks he could just distinguish several outbuildings he assumed belonged to Hollis. He'd known Doyle Withers since high school, and though he didn't figure the man for a liar, he thought it a bit handy that the perpetrator of this crime should be living a quarter mile from its scene. But, regardless of probability, an uneasiness began to grow as he went through the dense stand of trees, ducking branches, skirting thickets of thorn. When he came to the bottom of the hill, Martin unsnapped the strip of patent leather that lay over the hammer of his sidearm and loosened the weapon in its holster.

He emerged from the woods, walked into the clearing, and saw Hollis's home, only the front of it visible. Just above the door the ground rose and bled into the tree line, the rest of the structure dug back in the hill. There were a few round windows on one side of the door, a rectangular plate of glass on the other. A flagstone path led to the porch. Martin went up it and then, startled by a noise, turned to look behind him.

Twenty or thirty yards from where he stood was a small pen made of chain-link fencing. Inside, were several beagle puppies, a larger animal the deputy took for their mother. When the dogs saw Martin, they began barking, a shrill noise that sent tremors along his skin. He stood watching the animals for a few moments and then walked toward the house.

The door was made of solid oak. Martin gave a quick succession of raps with his knuckles, waited awhile, then knocked again. No sound came from inside. The dogs continued barking.

Stepping into the flowerbed, he made his way carefully among the rows of iris and azalea, moving across to the large bay window. He cupped his hands to either side of his eyes to block the glare and peered into the house. Through the glass was a long room in which the only furniture was a blue recliner and a small wooden table. There was no television, no stereo or electrical appliance. Against the walls, stacked almost to the ceiling, were brick and board bookshelves, on them rocks and sticks and various items one might find in the surrounding woods: pine-cone and spores, hornets' nests, and bits of shale. In the spaces between the bookshelves, Martin saw that Hollis had hung an assortment of leaves, all of them dipped in lacquer, framed in oak.

There was nothing inherently bizarre about any of these articles, but their cumulative effect on Martin caused him to back away from the window and glance nervously around him. He was not yet convinced that Hollis had killed the dog, but the beagles, coupled with what he'd seen of the man's home and the fact he was nowhere around, didn't speak to his innocence. Looking over, he saw that next to the house were tire tracks, a patch of faded grass that looked to be where a vehicle normally sat. Martin jotted a few notes, went down the flagstone path, and started up the hill.

Withers was inside the church when Martin made it back to the building. He climbed the steps, went through the double doors and into a small office where the deacon sat rifling through papers, placing currency into stacks, and stamping the backs of checks. The deacon saw Martin out of the corner of one eye and motioned him over to the desk, holding up a hand to let the deputy know he was in the middle of counting. As he finished, he leaned back in his chair and looked at Martin.

"Well," he asked, "what did Mr. Hollis have to say?"

Martin sat down on the far corner of the desk. "He wasn't home."

"Is that right?"

The deputy scratched at his cheek. "He's got a pen full of dogs down there, Doyle."

Withers raised his eyebrows. "Beagles?"

Martin nodded.

"You're telling me that sick so-and-so nailed up one of his own dogs?"

Martin crossed his arms. "We don't know that. Most the people out here have beagles. For all we know, some drunk teenager from Maud thought he'd drive over and play a prank. What I need to figure out is how much longer you guys plan on holding your little camp meeting."

The deacon's eyes narrowed. "Well," he said, "we talked about shutting our 'little camp meeting' down this weekend. I mentioned something to Brother Leslie about it last night."

"Yeah."

"But with this—" Withers broke off and gestured toward the roadside—"I think we'd be waving the white flag if we broke off now."

"How's that?" Martin asked.

"You know how these things get around. Soon as

187

you get someone out here to take that dog down, everybody in Perser will be talking about it. With Pastor Hassler getting sick on us and having to leave, the revival's all that's holding this church together." Withers shook his head and glanced out the window.

"Well," said Martin, "you know I can't make you all shut down. But if this Hollis character is the nut you say he is, I'm not sure if it's the best idea to be up here raising a ruckus every night. You don't know what someone like that—"

"Arrest him," Withers told the deputy. "Have one of your boys waiting to throw him in jail soon as he gets home. Get that big fella—what's his name—Lemming. Get Dave Lemming out here."

"I can't do that."

"Why?"

"Because we're not sure Hollis did anything. We're going to have to dust for prints, find out who the dog belongs to, question the neigh—You know how these things go, Doyle, you've seen *Cops*."

The longer he spoke, the more Withers's expression began to tighten. By the time Martin finished, his mouth was a thin, straight line.

Withers put rubber bands around the money and paper-clipped the checks, zipped everything into a First National bag. "Yeah," he said, standing and gathering his things, "I know exactly how these things go."

EVENING FOUND MARTIN stretched in front of his television. He and his wife had divorced a few years prior, and he'd given her most of the furniture. Martin kept only his recliner, but an important-looking bolt had recently appeared beneath the footrest and he felt unsafe tilting it back. Lying on the floor in the flickering blue light, his lower back just beginning to knot, he decided when he got up the next morning he'd disassemble the chair until he found what the bolt was meant to be attached to. He was looking forward to having the weekend off.

The day had taken its toll. Though Martin often complained about the dull nature of the calls he received, he'd realized for some time that he could not have endured it any other way. Some years back, he'd moved up north to a suburb of Minneapolis and taken a job with the U.S. Marshal Service. After several months, he was overwhelmed. It wasn't as if he'd been unaware of the type of crime that went on—it was the sheer enormity of what he saw that made him resentful. Not disheartened or insecure concerning his abilities, but angry, righteously indignant. He did not blame the perpetrators so much as the residents and the city itself—that vast network of lights, concrete, and noise—an entity that seemed to constantly produce the things that destroyed it. It spoke something of a town that there could be three homicides, a rape, and countless robberies any given night. Martin could not help feeling that anyone foolish and lazy enough to allow such things to happen had very nearly deserved them.

So, over the years, Perser had come to mean something quite particular to the deputy. He didn't much care if the rest of the country, or even the rest of the state, fell into disarray, as long as Perser, the boring, stale, weary little town he grew up in, stayed exactly as he'd known it. This was what had upset him about Jacob Hollis, the fact that by all accounts he was an outsider causing unnecessary trouble. He'd not let on in front of the deacon—the man was excitable enough without further agitating him— but Martin was much less calm than he presented himself. Unlike Withers, he hadn't already tried, convicted, and sentenced Hollis, but he couldn't help recognizing there was a part of him that would have enjoyed nothing better than to jail this Easterner, hassle him until he moved back to where he came from.

He flipped channels for several hours and had just started on his fifth beer when the phone rang. Martin glanced at his watch, saw it was nine thirty-seven, and thought about letting the machine answer. Rolling onto his knees, he made it to his feet and retrieved the phone on what sounded like its final ring. The voice on the other end was that of Sheriff Casteel. He said there had been another disturbance.

Martin lived in a housing addition eight miles

from the First Pentecostal, but it took him less time to cover the distance than it did to dress himself. When he pulled into the parking lot, he saw there were already two patrol cars in front of the building, a mass of men and women standing around the porch. An ambulance sat at the far end of the church; paramedics were loading an old woman onto a gurney.

The deputy parked beside the ambulance, took up his flashlight, and walked over to where Sheriff Casteel was addressing a group of churchgoers. Passing Deputy Lemming's car, he noticed they had placed a large, sandy-haired gentleman in the backseat. The man had a full beard, and Martin saw he had to rest his chin on his chest to keep his head from brushing the car's roof. In the constricted posture, his hands cuffed behind him and his eyes forced to his lap, he looked to be praying.

Casteel turned to face Martin just as he walked up. His khaki shirt was drenched and he seemed to be catching his breath. Martin looked over toward the ambulance and saw that Lemming was squatting against it with his head back, a bloodied rag held to his nostrils. Several paramedics were kneeling beside him tending to cuts on the man's face.

"Well," the sheriff told him, "you missed more excitement than I've seen in a while. I get you out of bed?"

"No," said Martin, "I was awake." He pointed over toward the ambulance. "What happened?"

Casteel fumbled in his shirt pocket for cigarettes, lit one, and took a long drag. "I'm still trying to figure that out."

The paramedics shut the ambulance doors, and the rig pulled onto the highway, it sirens springing suddenly to life. The vehicle receded behind the hill toward town.

"Sounds like these people were right about Hollis," said the sheriff. "Apparently, he came up here about a half hour ago and got into a scuffle with some of the men. That woman they just carted off is the evangelist's grandmother. She got knocked down the steps."

"Hollis knocked her down?"

"We're not really sure, but it took four of us to pry him off Lemming. They say he might have a minor concussion." Casteel shook his head and exhaled a long jet of smoke. "I thought Hollis was going to kill him."

Martin glanced over at the man sitting in the back of the patrol car. "He looks pretty sedate to me."

"Yeah," Casteel told him, "they get that way when you hit them with four or five tasers."

"Jesus."

"Probably what he's thinking."

Martin turned and saw that Doyle Withers was talking to a young, blond man on the porch. The deacon looked up, noticed the deputy, and began walking across the parking lot. Withers's shirt was ripped and his tie dangled out of his rear pocket. His hair, normally slicked with careful strokes, was hanging about his face.

"Hey," he called in a voice rife with vindication, "reckon you'd come out and give us a hand?"

"Thought about it," Martin told him, realizing he'd taken a dislike to the man. "The hell happened?"

"Well," said Withers, crossing his arms and gesturing toward Lemming's car with his chin, "like I already told the sheriff here, about forty-five minutes ago we were up at the altars having prayer, winding up the service and the rest of it, and all of a sudden I hear this commotion. Raised my head just in time to see Hollis come storming down the aisle, yelling 'Beagle this' and 'Beagle that,' and 'What'd you sorry blankety-blanks do to my dog?' Brother Paul walked up and tried to talk to him and he pushed Paulie over one of the pews and started in screaming."

Withers paused for a moment, cleared his throat. Martin found himself wishing he'd waited at Hollis's home until the man had returned.

"Next thing I knew, Duke and Brother Johnny had took hold of him. They drug him back up the aisle, got him outside, and that's when Hollis went in swinging. The church was emptied by then and Sister Snodgrass was standing right up front like she does. Hollis pushed Johnny over into her and down she goes, ends up at the bottom of the steps. It's only the Lord's good grace she didn't break her neck."

"So Hollis didn't attack the woman directly."

Withers looked at the deputy in disbelief. "No," he said. "He didn't attack her *directly*. What's that matter?"

Martin sighed, looked briefly at his feet. "I don't suppose it does."

"I don't suppose it does either," Withers told him. "Now you listen to me, Gerald. You'd arrested that man like I told you to, we wouldn't have had to go through all this. Sister Delores wouldn't be on her way to the hospital, bless her heart."

"I know," the deputy muttered.

"Well," said Withers. He ran a hand across his forehead and gave Martin a slap on the shoulder. "The important thing is we got him. With this and the dog, he might even get himself a trip to McAlester."

Martin shook his head. "I'll swing by tomorrow to check in on you all."

"You don't have to—"

"I'll swing by tomorrow," Martin told him.

He talked a bit longer with Casteel, asked him if he needed anything, and then began walking to his car. Considering the deacon's words, he blamed himself for not taking Hollis into custody earlier that day. As he passed the man, he couldn't even look in his direction. Instead, he focused his attention on the moon that had just lately risen, squatting at the horizon like a pustule waiting to burst.

MARTIN GOT VERY little sleep that night. When he climbed out of bed early the next morning, he called down to the hospital to check on Mrs. Snodgrass. The woman, he was told, had been treated for a broken ankle and would be released later in the day. Lemming, on the other hand, would have to be held at least seventy-two hours for observation. His concussion had turned out to be less minor than they'd thought.

The deputy switched off his phone and sat holding the receiver. From where he was, he could see the recliner, the bolt he'd laid on one of its arms. Standing, he went into the living room and began to disassemble it.

That evening he drove out to the First Pentecostal. There were a number of cars in the parking lot, several men sitting around the front steps balancing paper plates on their laps. He got out of his car and walked across the churchyard, the noise of cicadas swelling up from a field to the east.

Inside, he found the congregation seated in the fellowship hall, most of them occupied with eating. From across the room he saw Doyle Withers raise a hand and wave. Martin went over and took the spot beside him.

The two talked for a few minutes, and when Martin inquired about Mrs. Snodgrass, Withers offered to introduce him to the woman and her grandson. They got up and walked to the head of one of the tables where a teenage boy sat loading portions of baked beans onto a plastic spoon. The boy was sickly looking, pale. His hands were small and his arms thin. He did not seem to Martin like he was capable of holding a conversation, much less a revival.

"Where's your grandmamma?" Withers asked.

The boy told them she was in the kitchen.

Martin followed the deacon around a corner and into a small kitchen where several women were preparing food. Over by one wall, crutches beneath both her arms, stood Delores Snodgrass, talking with the cooks, overseeing the making of dessert. The woman had silver hair and a strong, angular face, only a few wrinkles around her gray eyes and mouth. She was wearing a full-length dress, and her sleeves were pushed onto her forearms. Other than the crutches and a walking cast, there was no sign of anything having happened to her.

"Sister Snodgrass?"

The woman turned toward the men and smiled.

"I wanted to introduce you to someone," Withers said. "This is Deputy Martin. I've known him for twenty years. He's working on putting that Hollis in the penitentiary."

Mrs. Snodgrass swung her way over to the men, propped herself on the crutches, and extended a hand. Martin was surprised by the woman's grip.

"It's nice to know you, deputy."

"Good to meet you."

"Can we fix you a plate?"

"No ma'am, I can't talk but a minute."

"You're not staying for service?" she asked.

"Actually," he said, realizing the woman had somehow moved even closer to him, "they have to have me back at the station."

"I think you'd really enjoy hearing my Leslie preach."

Martin turned to Withers for help. The deacon's face had broken out in a grin.

"Well," he told her, "I really need to get back."

"Would you at least like some coffee?"

Martin said that he would.

Mrs. Snodgrass turned to the counter, poured coffee into a Styrofoam cup, and handed it to Martin. He, Withers, and the old woman went back to the fellowship hall and took seats next to the evangelist. They talked for a while about the revival, how long Leslie had been preaching. Soon, the boy excused himself from the table, saying he had to spend some time in prayer before service. Martin watched him unfold his dress coat from the chair beside him, put it on and walk carefully from the room. There was something about Snodgrass's voice that sharply countered the deputy's first opinion of him. He shook his head and laughed.

"That's about the politest young man I've seen in years."

"Thank you," said Mrs. Snodgrass.

"How old is he?"

"He'll be sixteen next March."

Martin sipped his coffee. "Are Mom and Dad here tonight?"

"No," said the woman, her face nearly expressionless. "It's just him and me. Has been since he was five years old."

The deputy nodded, said she'd done a fine job. Mrs. Snodgrass replied that the Lord had done a lot more to raise the boy than she had.

They talked longer and then Martin looked down to his coffee cup. He began telling the woman how sorry he was she'd been hurt. Smiling, she reached over and placed a hand atop the deputy's.

"I feel terrible about all of it," he continued, "about you falling and the dog—" He stopped, cleared his throat.

"Well," said the woman, withdrawing her hand, "I believe everything happens for a reason."

The deacon nodded in agreement.

"If I hadn't hurt my ankle, I probably wouldn't have gotten to meet you. And if that poor animal hadn't—well, it's awful, but, like Brother Withers

DOG ON THE CROSS

says, the revival would just have shut down that much sooner and there'd be a lot of people Leslie wouldn't have gotten to preach to. There might even have been someone lost over it." The woman looked at him intently. "Just think about that."

Martin found he wasn't able to think about it. All he could think of was Hollis, how he might ensure that serious charges were brought against the man.

The deputy shifted in his chair. "You and your grandson actually went down one day and talked with him?"

"Talked with who?"

"Jacob Hollis."

"Yes," said the woman, shaking her head. "I don't know how much good it did, but maybe we planted a seed. I always tell Leslie that—"

"Would you be willing to testify?"

"How's that?"

"Testify," Martin told her, "in court. There'll be a hearing and it would help us a lot if you could just talk about what he said to you that day."

Mrs. Snodgrass seemed frightened by this. She laid a hand to her breast. "I don't know," she said. "I've never even been inside a courthouse."

"It would be a huge help to us."

"Are you sure?"

"I'm positive," Martin said.

The woman paused to consider Martin's advice. Deacon Withers coughed into his fist.

"Anyway," said Martin, taking a final sip of his coffee, flattening the cup and stowing it in his pocket, "just give it some thought."

He rose from the table and picked his hat off the seat next to him, stood there holding it by the brim. "I suppose I ought to get," he said. "It's been real nice meeting you. Tell your grandson he's an impressive young man."

Mrs. Snodgrass lifted her head and gave the deputy a confused look. Judging by her expression, she hadn't believed he was going anywhere.

MARTIN ENDED UP sitting through song service—song service, offering, sermon, and altar call. When he finally had the opportunity to make an exit, his neck was stiff and his shoulder blades ached from being pressed into the pew. On his way out of the building, he met Mrs. Snodgrass in the foyer. She shook his hand and said she hoped to see him the following night. He told her he'd do his best to make it.

The next afternoon, he drove down to the station and found Sheriff Casteel pacing about his office. It was Martin's day off, but the fingerprint results were due sometime that evening and the deputy wanted to be there when they arrived. The lab report had not yet come in, but Hollis's lawyer had flown from Connecticut the night before. The sheriff said that this was what he'd feared all along: an Eastern attorney coming into town to create problems at pre-trial. For days he had tried to get Hollis to consent to an interview, but the man knew the Miranda warning all too well. His lawyer had told him to say nothing until he arrived. It was only a few hours prior, after having spoken with his attorney, that Jacob Hollis informed the sheriff he was willing to be interviewed. Standing there in his office with the case file laid open on the desk before him, Casteel asked if Martin would conduct the interrogation. He thought the deputy's experience in the marshall service might give him an advantage.

"We'll definitely get him on assault and battery," said the sheriff, "felony assault of an officer. But even then he might be able to get off with probation and a fine."

"He doesn't have any priors?" asked Martin.

"Nothing," Casteel told him. "If you can get him to talk about nailing that dog up, our chances get a lot better. Doesn't matter how liberal a jury they come up with. We show a few pictures of the beagle, prove that Hollis did it, we might could get him a couple a years in the state farm."

The deputy said he was probably right.

Upon his returning from Minneapolis, Martin had convinced the sheriff that his examination techniques were out of date. Having come of age in the fifties, Casteel continued to have a vision of rubber hoses and hot lights, officers standing over their suspects with rolled sleeves and cigarettes. All this meant was that what evidence Casteel was able to obtain was most always ruled inadmissible. Martin knew that in judicial procedure even the presence of handcuffs in the interrogation room could cause issues of coercion to arise.

So, while not thrilled about the prospect of interviewing Hollis, Martin agreed with the sheriff that he was probably best suited for the job. It would take a certain amount of effort to mask his anger and disgust, but the deputy knew the better he played the part of advocate, the better the chances Hollis would open up. He poured a fresh cup of coffee and asked that the man be brought to the room for questioning.

Daylight was just beginning to fail when Martin entered with his legal tablet and coffee. The blinds were open and he saw that a number of people were still going back and forth along the sidewalks of downtown, in and out of stores, across the north end of Linton Park. Hollis was sitting there turned toward the windows, his fingers twitching nervously. The lamps lent the walls a golden hue. Martin could hear cars passing on the street below them.

The deputy walked to the chair opposite Hollis and seated himself. This was the first decent look he'd had at the prisoner, and though his irritation diminished it, there was something about Hollis that unsettled him. Martin considered this as he looked over the outline he'd prepared earlier that afternoon. Hollis's face—bearded, framed with wire-rimmed glasses— seemed intelligent to the deputy, almost pleasant.

Martin introduced himself, asked the prisoner if he was comfortable, if he'd like something to drink. Hollis indicated he was fine.

"I want to tell you," said Martin, "I'm no friend of those crazies out there at that church, so you can say whatever you want to me."

Hollis nodded.

"Someone's explained your rights?"

He nodded again.

"You don't mind if I record our conversation?"

"No."

Martin pulled a small recorder from his pocket, reached over, and placed it on the coffee table in front of them. Pressing the red button, he positioned the microphone toward Hollis.

"Can you state your name again for me?"

The man crossed his arms to his chest, brushed at his chin. "Jacob Andrew Hollis."

"What's your address, Mr. Hollis?"

"Route 4, Box 236-P."

"How old are you?"

"Forty-seven."

"And where were you born, sir?"

"Baltimore."

Martin forced a smile. "Can you tell me about your education?"

"I have a B.S. in chemistry from the University of Vermont. I have a master's from Massachusetts."

"Chemistry?"

"Yes."

"What's your occupation?"

"I'm retired."

Martin smiled. "Must be nice," he said. "How you get the cash to retire in your forties, you don't mind my asking."

"I inherited some money when my parents passed away," Hollis told him. "I have a few patents as well."

"Chemical patents or—"

"Yes."

"This is your first arrest?"

"Yes."

"Any trouble with the law before that?"

"None," said Hollis.

"Any history of mental illness or depression?"

"I'd prefer not to answer that."

Martin wrote for a few moments. He looked up. "They been treating you all right?"

Hollis told them they had.

"Why'd you move to Perser, Mr. Hollis?"

It seemed as if the man hadn't understood what had been asked him.

"Mr. Hollis," said Martin, "why did you decide to move here?"

Hollis cleared his throat. He brushed his palms

across his cheeks and leaned back in his chair. His hands jittered.

"It's okay if you don't want to answer," said Martin.

Hollis shook his head. "I'm just not sure you would understand."

"Try me."

The man exhaled a long, slow breath. "I moved out here to be alone," he said. "I wanted to get away from the noise."

Martin sat his pen down for a moment.

"Noise?"

"Yes."

"You moved halfway across the country to get away from noise and ended up beside a Pentecostal church?"

Hollis looked toward the window. "I had no idea what *Pentecostal* meant back then. My uncle owned land out here when I was a child. When the realtor told me about acreage next to a church, being harassed night and day was the furthest thing from my mind."

Martin nodded, took up his pen and scribbled something. "So, that's what finally got to you?"

"What do you mean?"

"Just that it makes sense," said Martin.

"Just that what makes sense?"

"That you attacked those people, nailed up your dog. I'm sure it was hard for you. I'm sure you couldn't take their racket anymore and had to show them—"

"I didn't do anything to my dog," Hollis interrupted. "I've never harmed an animal in my life."

Martin gave the man a weak grin. "Everyone has a breaking point, don't they, Jacob? You mind if I call you Jacob?"

Hollis said that he didn't.

"I can't tell you some of the things I've done because of—"

"I didn't hurt my dog."

The deputy looked at him. "Do you have any idea who might've?"

"It was one of them."

"One of who?" Martin asked.

"The church members," said Hollis. "They came down and—" The man broke off and stared down at his feet. He ran a hand through his hair.

Martin wrote for a while. He asked Hollis if he could prove any of this.

Hollis continued staring at the floor.

"You can't prove it can you, Jacob?"

"Of course I can't."

"Then why would you expect me to believe it?"

"I don't."

Martin scribbled this onto the tablet.

"But whether you believe it or not," said Hollis, "those people despise me. They're tired of my complaining."

"What's there to complain about?"

"Their music."

"How can you hear their music in an underground home with the windows and doors shut and the air conditioner on?"

"I just can," Hollis told him. "Noise like that gives me nausea. During service, the sound of their bass travels down through the hill. I can see it vibrating the water in my sink. That's why I went up there the first time. I just went up to ask if they could be quieter."

Martin listened to this, wanting to feel that he were making progress, that the man was nearing a confession of his guilt. But the longer Hollis spoke, the more there grew a suspicion he was, at least partially, telling the truth. Martin tried to force it back, to remind himself of what the congregation had been through, of Deputy Lemming in the hospital bed, Mrs. Snodgrass's crutches. He pictured her standing there in front of him and for a moment pushed his doubt away.

"You know you sent an old woman to the hospital," he said.

"I realize that."

"A very sweet woman."

Hollis looked up at him. "I can't say I'm entirely sorry."

Martin stared at him for a moment and then broke out laughing—partly because of the extremity of the man's statement, partly because it reassured him of Hollis's guilt. Recovering, he shook his head.

"Aren't you a sweetheart?" Martin said.

"Have you spoken to her, Mr. Martin?"

"I have," said the deputy, putting down his tablet. "And I'll tell you, all I could think was how horrible it was someone decided to knock her down a flight of steps. She's almost seventy, Jacob. You're lucky you're not facing manslaughter."

Hollis looked off into space for a while. "She and her grandson came down to my house one day."

"She told me."

"They came down, knocked on my door, and for some reason I let them in."

The deputy sipped his coffee.

"I tried to tell them I wasn't interested in converting, but that woman kept on and on. She said I had no choice but to come to their service. She said that refusal to attend the words of the Lord's anointed was a blasphemy punishable by hellfire. That's what she called her grandson, Mr. Martin—'the Lord's anointed.'"

The deputy wasn't impressed with this.

"I remember he noticed I had beagle puppies and asked if I would sell him one."

"There's nothing wrong with that boy," warned Martin.

"I never said there was," Hollis told him. "He seemed like a sweet child. If I'm remembering it right, he never got to say a word the entire time he was in my house."

"He's shy."

"It's not the boy that worries me."

"Why even bring him up?"

"Because his grandmother's using him."

"*Using* him?"

"Yes."

"Using him for what?"

"I don't know," said Hollis. "Attention, fame—I couldn't really say. But I do know if it were up to her that revival would go on for the rest of their lives." He stopped for a moment and stared back out the window. "I believe that's why she killed my dog."

Martin found he wanted to laugh at this as well. He opened his mouth to let out a snicker, but one never came.

Later, this would remind him of the first time he was struck in a fight. He was barely ten years old at the time and a boy on the playground had hit him squarely in the center of his forehead. For a few seconds, Martin had stood there looking at his attacker in disbelief. He'd always imagined a punch would feel much differently, imagined it would immediately hurt. It was not until Martin was dragged into the principal's office for shoving the boy down an embankment that he felt the onset of a headache that lasted for most of the week.

Similarly, Hollis's words had made no initial

impression. They seemed the type of nonsense that the mentally disturbed will blather under duress. Then, slowly, the tenor of the words shifted. After a few moments had passed, Martin felt as if a lump were swelling on his forehead. He told Hollis he should watch his mouth.

"Why do I need to—"

"Because you're crazy," Martin said flatly. He knew he should go out into the hall and collect himself, but he did not budge.

Hollis leaned forward and sat with his elbows on his knees. "No, Mr. Martin, I'm not. You know I'm not."

The deputy wanted to say something in reply, but he couldn't think of what. His mind was going very fast.

"I'll go ahead and tell you what I believe happened," said Hollis, "since you seem to be the only person around here who's willing to listen." The man looked to make sure the recorder was going. "I was in Tulsa all last week attending a conference at TU; you can confirm that if you want. When I got back into town Friday afternoon, I stopped for gas at the four-mile and there were two men behind the counter talking about a dog getting nailed to the cross out at the First Pentecostal. I had no idea it was even my dog they were talking about, but I remember thinking immediately that it was the old woman who did it."

Martin began shaking his head.

"That's why I went up there and lost it, deputy. I came home, saw my dog was missing, and knew what had happened. I couldn't help myself. I knew she'd done it to make it look like they were under attack. I knew she'd done it to keep her revival going."

Martin scooted forward in his chair. "You're telling me that a seventy-year-old woman—an elder in a Pentecostal church—stole your dog, carried it two hundred yards and hammered it to a cross with sixteen-penny nails?"

"That's exactly what I'm telling you."

"Have you ever driven a sixteen-penny nail, Mr. Hollis?"

"No, but I've shaken hands with that woman and felt her grip. Have you shaken her hand, deputy?"

"You want to know what?" he asked the man. "You're just about to piss me—"

"Maybe she had an accomplice. I'm sure a revival gets fairly lucrative after a month's worth of services. I'm sure there's someone who stands to make—"

The deputy found he couldn't listen to any more of this. He yelled at the man to stop. "Just quit," he told him. "You don't have a scrap of evidence. You're talking right out your ass."

"Deputy," resumed Hollis in a calm voice, "it's good you're getting upset. But you need to ask yourself why you're upset. I think it's because you know I'm telling the truth. I think it's because you don't want—"

Martin reached over and switched off the recorder. "If you don't shut your goddamned mouth, I'm going to have the boys bring in one of those tasers you're so fond of." He glared at the man and, then standing, left the room, slamming the door so hard that the wall trembled. He looked down the hall and saw Deputy Jackson sitting there, a curious expression on his face.

"You got what you need?" he asked.

Martin nodded inadvertently, gestured toward the room. Jackson went inside, told Hollis to stand, placed handcuffs on him and walked him out. Martin watched the two descend the stairs and then went back and eased himself into the chair. He sat for a long time looking out the window, backing the recorder, and listening to sections of their conversation.

When he went downstairs, Casteel was standing at the front desk talking with the dispatch. The sheriff held a large brown envelope, and seeing Martin, he began to motion him over.

"Lab report just came in," he said. "Those prints don't belong to Hollis or anybody else they've arrested in Oklahoma in the last forty-five years."

Martin felt as if he were going to be ill.

"That doesn't necessarily mean anything," Casteel told him. "I'm sure he's smart enough to've worn gloves. We don't have to have the prints to convict him of aggravated assault and resisting arrest."

The sheriff raised his coffee mug and took a long drink.

Watching him, his face drained of color, Martin told the man he'd be back in a moment. He went out to his car, dug around the front seat, and found the cup he'd accidentally taken from church the night before. Carrying it inside, he pitched it to Casteel.

"What's this?" the man asked, studying the flattened piece of Styrofoam. "You feeling okay?"

Martin didn't answer. He walked down the hallway and into the bathroom. Even the sheriff, deaf as he was, had no trouble hearing the sound the bolt made when the deputy shot it to behind him.

SEVERAL WEEKS LATER, Jacob Hollis pleaded guilty to assault charges and paid fifty-seven hundred dollars in fines. He sold his home to a Dutch family at the end of summer and, much to the liking of the First Pentecostal, moved back to New England. Hollis didn't appear in court for the civil suit filed against him by Doyle Withers, and Judge Petersen issued a bench warrant should the man come back through Oklahoma. He told Withers, however, not to hold his breath. The judge didn't expect Hollis would be eager to revisit the state.

It was also along this time that the church brought its camp meeting to an end. The revival, said the elders of the congregation, was the longest they'd heard of, services every day for two and a half months.

Leslie Snodgrass and his grandmother moved out of their hotel room and went back to the even smaller town outside Tishomingo. When the United Pentecostal Board of Churches sent in a new pastor, a Virginian by the name of Don Shockley, Mrs. Snodgrass wrote a letter of protest to the UPBC chairman. She had hoped her grandson could apply for the post and felt he hadn't been given proper consideration. Hearing of the letter, Reverend Shockley phoned to see if the boy would be interested in preaching the next summer. The woman told him she would think about it.

Gerald Martin found himself in the process of moving as well. In December of that year, he resigned the office of deputy sheriff and took a position as fire watcher in central Colorado. Standing on the balcony of his tower and looking out over the miles of evergreen, he could, at times, convince himself he'd made the right decision. The foothills of the Rocky Mountains lay on the horizon, and the air was clean and crisp. But every evening, as the sun declined and stained the western windows, Martin felt that a hollowness had grown inside him, and while eager for companionship, he didn't know if he could return to suburban or even rural life. He thought he must be looking for a different community altogether.

The day he'd resigned, Casteel had wanted to know why he was losing his best deputy, why, in his opinion, Martin was throwing away a promising career in law enforcement. The wide receiver for the football team had been missing since the end of summer—Casteel might need assistance with that—and, after all, didn't Martin understand he had an opportunity to be sheriff himself in a few years? The deputy simply shook his head in answer to such questions, but when Casteel wanted to know who it was had handed him that Styrofoam cup, Martin told him flatly that he didn't remember. The sheriff attempted to jog his memory, using as incentive the fact that the prints on the cup had proven a perfect match with the ones on the nails. Martin said he'd like to help, but it seemed such a trivial thing at the time, there was no way he was going to recall it.

Casteel merely shrugged. He was just glad Hollis was no longer his problem. "Let those Easterners deal with him," he told Martin. "They're used to nuts like that. It's so bad out there, they can't tell the priests from the perverts." Martin said the perverts were better received.

But his flippancy aside, this was the type of concern that Martin devoted an increasing amount of thought to. For much of his life, he'd had an unwavering sense of right and wrong—their origin, what distinguished them, the things on which they fed. He'd chosen to think that evil arose from without, that only the man who entertained it was in any real danger. Now it was otherwise with Martin, and while he understood that to some this might be an epiphany that fostered tolerance and wisdom, the former deputy simply felt unbalanced by the realization, as if one of the legs of his tower had been sawed away and the structure was subject to collapse.

Lying on his cot at night, he would sometimes dream of the old woman. He would not see her as she'd been in life, but rather as something fantastical, a figure gnarled and distorted, a fairy-book crone. Stalking the hills in her gingham dress, a gunnysack hoisted over one shoulder, she'd move beneath the oak limbs with a face that admitted no cruelty, no hatred or malice, stopping at times to reach into the sack and assure the whimpering thing that flailed inside it. Most nights, she would perform her duties alone, holding firmly the muzzle as she applied strips of duct tape, grasping the torso as she drove the nails. But there were others when Martin would find himself standing beside her—helping the woman, to the best of his ability, carry out her task. Sometimes words of comfort would escape her lips, but Martin could never quite catch them, and he knew that in any case, they were not for him.

Awakening from these dreams, he might think for a moment he could hear something knocking against the legs of his tower, scratching at the support beams. He would stumble to the balcony and peer over the ledge, wishing to see some beast he could draw aim on with the pistol he continued to keep with him. But the sounds proved only the wind in the treetops, their branches thrashing below him, no monsters visible in that sea of black.

ACKNOWLEDGMENTS

I WOULD LIKE TO extend my sincere appreciation to my agent, Nat Sobel, and my editor, Kathy Pories, for all their guidance. Thanks also to my grandparents, Ruth and Jerry Martin, without whose love and support I never would have made it; to Dr. Robert Hill, who started me on this path (whether he'll own up to it or not); and to my friends Mark Walling and Clint Stewart, readers extraordinaire, whose comments on the manuscript kept me honest and whose friendship kept me sane. "The Offering" is in tribute to the remarkable Susan Tyler, who, unlike the protagonist of my story, continues to astonish family and friends with her courage, strength, and wisdom.